THE BOOK OF NEIL

a novel by Frank Turner Hollon

THE BOOK OF NEIL

a novel by Frank Turner Hollon

MACADAM CAGE

MacAdam/Cage
155 Sansome Street, Suite 550
San Francisco, CA 94104
www.macadamcage.com

Library of Congress Cataloging-in-Publication Data

Hollon, Frank Turner, 1963-
The Book of Neil / by Frank Turner Hollon.
pages cm
ISBN 978-1-59692-385-0 (hardcover)
1. Second Advent—Fiction. I. Title.
PS3608.O494B68 2012
813'.6—dc23
2012040515

Book and cover design by Dorothy Carico Smith

*Do not forget to entertain strangers, for by so doing
some have unwittingly entertained angels.*

—Hebrews (13:2)

NEIL 1:1

THE FIRST TIME I SAW JESUS was on the fourteenth hole of Crystal Creek golf course on a Friday afternoon around 3:30.

He was part of a threesome ahead of us, and from a distance I could see him on the tee box wearing a greyish robe tied by a thick rope around the waist. His hair was long and swept across his shoulders with each practice swing.

I tried not to stare.

On the sixteenth hole, my playing partner, Earl, got a call from his office and had to abandon me. On the seventeenth tee, overlooking a short par three with the oblong green surrounded by water on both sides, I caught up to the group ahead stopping my golf cart a respectful distance behind as they each hit their approach shots.

The first man, at least eighty years old, shanked his shot left and short but didn't seem to mind much. The next guy, a fattish teenager with a puffy face and fluid swing, sailed a six iron just past the flag and spun the ball back within two feet. Golf has no conscience.

JESUS STEPPED UP TO THE TEE. It looked like a five iron in his hand. He was very deliberate over the ball, moving his left foot a few inches and then back again, pressing his large hands forward in silence.

It was one of those weird backswings, kinda herky-jerky, slow on the rise and quick through the zone. I was surprised to see the ball come off the face of the club at such a steep angle, flying higher than the fat kid's shot despite the club difference.

Jesus seemed pleased with the results. He turned to me and politely asked if I wanted to join the group for the remaining two holes. I put my clubs on the back of his cart and Jesus drove.

His sandals were old and worn, and he had a peculiar odor. The old man and the teenager veered off the cart path to the left. We stopped under a tree to watch the old man's shot.

Jesus said, "You're probably wondering what I'm doing here."

I didn't answer. It didn't seem necessary.

"I'm playing golf," he said. "A frustrating game. I don't really have the patience for it, but I enjoy playing anyway."

We sat quietly and watched the old man exit the golf cart and select a club from his bag. He put the club back in the bag and got a different one, looking up at the treetops for signs of wind direction.

"How do you know those guys?" I asked, making conversation, keeping my eyes on the other cart.

"I don't. They put us together on the first tee. The old man's Jewish. The kid doesn't recognize me."

The fat teenager had his attention transfixed on a cell phone six inches from his face, reading a tiny important message.

"I need to ask you a question, Neil," he said.

It didn't seem peculiar he knew my name. It was written on the scorecard. "Okay," I answered.

Jesus asked, "Have you ever robbed a bank?"

It wasn't the question I expected, although I'm not sure I could have told you beforehand what question I did expect.

"No," I said, as the old man swung his nine iron almost completely missing the ball. The teenager never moved his eyes from the cell phone as the old man addressed the ball again, looking back and forth from the red flag waving on the pin to the mystical white ball at his feet.

"Why would you ask whether I'd robbed a bank?"

"I don't keep a scorecard," Jesus said. "In golf, I mean. I used to, but it just made me anxious. Because you know what? I can't stop myself from keeping up with the score in my head. Right now I could tell you what I got on every hole, and what the kid shot, and even the old man."

The teenager leaned over a putt while his cell phone vibrated in the pocket of his khaki shorts. The ball ran up to the hole, stopped on the precipice, and dropped gently away for a birdie. The kid could barely bend over enough to retrieve it from the bottom of the cup.

"Nice putt," I said.

He didn't look at me, and I noticed some mustard on his meaty chin. Maybe it wasn't mustard, but it was yellow, nonetheless.

The old man made a seven. I dropped a ten foot putt for par. Jesus clapped.

Back in the cart on the ride to the last tee box, I said again, "Why did you ask me if I'd ever robbed a bank?"

He answered matter-of-factly, "You've wanted to be rich all your life, right? Imagine the thousands and thousands of hours you've spent thinking about money, and what you could do with it, and how it could solve all of your problems. You've even prayed for it, Neil."

We pulled alongside the eighteenth tee. The goofy teenager answered a call on the way from his cart to the box.

"Yeah," he said. "Playin' golf."

There was a pause as we all waited for him to lean over and place the ball on a tee. The kid seemed to have no concept his telephone conversation was causing any inconvenience.

"I don't know," he mumbled. And then, "That's stupid…okay…somewhere in the closet."

Jesus whispered to me as he stared at the teenager like he was trying to figure out something about the boy. "So why haven't you robbed a bank? If you think money will solve your problems, and the bank has lots of money, it seems logical you'd rob a bank. Every reward has a risk, and with good planning you could minimize the risk."

"I don't know if that's such a good idea," I said.

A few minutes later Jesus hit a fantastic approach

shot into the 18th green. The ball skirted the middle trap and circled to the back hole location. From where I stood it looked like it may have ticked the pin on the way by.

As we sat and watched the old man skull the ball into the trunk of an oak tree, I asked, "How long have you been back?"

"Quite a while actually, but nobody seems to notice. Maybe I waited too long."

"What do you mean?" I asked.

"We've got a country full of Christians who proclaim they've been waiting patiently for me to return for two thousand years, and when I finally come back, nobody believes it."

He continued, "I spent three days in jail in Topeka, Kansas, for violating a loitering ordinance because I was preaching too long at a street corner. A Probate Court in Alabama declared me mentally incompetent, and I spent thirty days in a rather bad place. Walking down the interstate outside Los Angeles somebody hit me in the back of the head with a sandwich.

"I've been cussed at, laughed at, shot at, and a lady in Philadelphia spit in my face for the sacrilege of impersonating the Savior. But you know what, Neil? Not one person has asked me for forgiveness. Not one person has asked me to save them."

I really didn't know what to say. Jesus seemed sad, but mostly he seemed confused by it all.

"Maybe I waited too long, Neil," he said. "People seem to have other gods now, like computers, cell phones, new cars, or even their own tight and tan bodies. I've seen athletes worshipped by children. Movie stars, politicians, even people who sing poorly. Worshipped, admired, emulated. And yet people go to church on Sundays, and call themselves Christians, and justify their false gods the minute they walk out the church doors to their wasteful meals, ridiculous large-screen televisions, and indulgent lives."

Jesus missed his three-foot birdie putt. He appeared distracted. The fat kid carded a 72, and as we parted ways with the other cart I watched him placing his cell phone gently in a special maroon velvet pouch.

Jesus drove the cart into the parking lot and came to a stop behind my car.

"So let's rob a bank, Neil," he said. "You might not fully understand why I would do such a thing, but it's something I need to do. Maybe I'll get some press out of it. The Jesus Bandit. Good story. Who knows, maybe they'll pay attention."

I listened with skepticism.

Jesus explained, "And you'll get rich, Neil. You can join this country club you and your wife have wanted so badly to join. And she can have a new car. The car she drives now embarrasses her, you know."

"I know," I said weakly.

We sat quietly for several minutes. I thought about everything he'd said, and I wondered why this man, Jesus or not, would choose me.

"Why did you pick me?" I asked.

"You picked yourself," he said. "I just asked if you wanted to join our threesome. The rest is healthy coincidence, if you believe in such things."

NEIL 1:2

I DIDN'T MENTION THE MEETING WITH Jesus to my wife, Amanda.

"How'd you play?" she asked, disinterested.

"Not very well. Earl ended up leaving after the six-teenthth hole. I don't think he understands golf. The primary purpose of the game is to get outside and get away from everything. Why bring a cell phone? It's kinda like bringing a lawnmower to a movie theater. You might as well stay home and cut the grass."

It should be noted that my wife has an unquench-able need for more. More money. More square feet of living space. More shoes. More everything. The un-quenchable need appears to be inbred. A deep animal instinct of survival perverted by civilization.

It makes sense for a mother grizzly bear to want

the most salmon for herself and her cubs, or the safest cave in the whole forest, but we're so far removed from actual survival, the female instinct to have more and more translates now to a closet filled with seventy-seven pairs of shoes. Seventy-seven. Or a house so big certain rooms are almost never entered. And dogs with sweaters. Or a new car every two years regardless of the previous car's performance. A freezer full of food, most of it destined for a trash can.

"Why would anyone bring a lawnmower to a movie theater?" she asked wistfully.

"Where are the kids?" I asked.

"Upstairs. Gina needs two hundred and fifty dollars for this Saturday's soccer tournament. Prom is next weekend. Elise picked out a dress. It's only five hundred and thirty dollars, which is a good deal if you ask me."

"Why don't they get jobs?" I wondered out loud.

My wife turned and looked at me like I'd suggested the girls quit school and become street whores.

"Don't be stupid. They're in high school."

"What's your point?" I asked.

"Life will be tough enough. They should enjoy themselves as long as possible."

"They sit around all day eatin' cookies, talkin' on the phone, and watching TV."

"Exactly," she said.

I explained, "It's like sayin' everybody has to run a marathon next year, so instead of training to succeed, instead of getting prepared, we should all sleep late, get fat, and do nothing, because that marathon is gonna be a bitch and we need to rest up for it."

She listened to my explanation.

"Exactly," she said again, with annoying finality.

"Maybe we could sell a few of your shoes to pay for Gina's soccer tournament," I suggested.

She responded, "Maybe you could stop playing golf twice a month and use the money for your family."

"And maybe you could get a job," I said quickly.

Her laugh was instantaneous, which was perhaps more insulting than the laugh itself. When it ended, she said, "You can't make me."

I was finally able to say, "What?"

"You can't make me. Are you gonna make me fill out applications? Are you gonna make me sit through job interviews?"

I hadn't thought of it that way. Standing in the kitchen, staring at the unpleasant face of my wife, robbing a bank didn't seem like such a bad idea.

NEIL 1:3

THE SECOND TIME I SAW JESUS he was sitting outside a gas station eating a bag of Doritos, Cool Ranch.

I stopped in front of him. "What are you doing here?"

"Why does everybody have to attach such spiritual significance to everything I do? I'm eating Doritos. That's all. Have you been thinking about the bank?"

I lowered my voice. "Yes, I have."

Jesus stood and threw the snack bag in a nearby trash can. "Let's take a ride in your car and I'll tell you about it."

Heading east on a country road, Jesus said, "People are always asking me how the world will end. I read in the newspaper they added another second to the atomic clock. It's the thirty-first second added since the early 1970s. It's done to compensate for a slowing of the Earth's rotation. In other words, the planet will slow down until it stops all together. When it does, with one side in total darkness and one side in total light, everybody will rush to the edges. You can go a few miles in one direction to grow crops and spend the day in the sun, and then a few miles in the other direction to sleep and enjoy the nightlife."

I asked, "Is that the way the world will end, slowly coming to a stop?"

"I don't think so," he said, looking out the window at a field of cows. "Do you have a gun?" he asked.

"Yes," I confessed.

"Why?"

He asked the question, but I was convinced that he already knew the answer. There didn't seem much point in lying.

So I said, "In case I can't stand living in this world another single minute."

"Where is it?" he asked.

"Under your seat."

Jesus reached beneath and pulled out the pistol. He turned it over in his hand several times before saying, "Man is born to trouble, as the sparks fly upward."

We rode along in silence for a while.

Jesus said, "Here's the plan. Tomorrow morning I'll meet you in the little wooded area behind Crescent Bank. Park your car in the Wal-Mart lot, far away from any parking lot cameras. Walk around the back at 9:15 in the morning. Bring your gun, but don't load it."

As he spoke, Jesus stared out the front window. His lips seemed dry.

"Do you need some ChapStick?"

He turned to me. "No, thank you."

Then he continued, "Go to a Goodwill store this afternoon in another town. Get a pair of reading glasses and a baseball cap, along with oversized clothes you wouldn't usually wear. Stuff something in your shirt to make you look bigger on camera. Bring a change of clothes in your car."

I listened to his plan.

"Have you ever done this before?"

"No," he said, and then explained, "You go in the bank first and get in line. When I come in afterward, everyone will stare at me. That's what they do, stare at me.

"I'll explain to the people it's a robbery and show the gun. I'll pretend you're just a regular customer and demand the teller fill the bag with money. No dye packs or alarms.

"When I point the gun at you, put your hands up and act scared. I'll order you to take the bag from the teller and follow me to the door, making sure to explain you'll be my hostage in case anything goes wrong.

"When we get to the door, you break free from me and take off outside like you're getting away from a psychopath. Run through the woods, and then slow down walking through the parking lot to your car. Don't look anyone in the face. Drive your car to the grocery store two blocks away. Park in a location where you can change clothes in the car without being noticed.

"After you've changed clothes, throw the baseball cap, glasses, and Goodwill clothes in the dumpster behind the grocery store. Bury the money tomorrow night in the yard."

It wasn't as odd as I thought it would be, listening to Jesus describe robbing a bank.

"What will you do?" I asked.

"I'll stay in the bank long enough for you to get away. Then I'll just wait until the police arrive. I'll insist I was working alone and my hostage got away carrying the money and foiled the entire plan."

"What about the gun?" I asked.

"What do you mean?"

"It'll be traced back to me."

"I don't know much about guns. Where can we get one that can't be traced?"

I thought about it. "I have an old pellet gun pistol that looks exactly like a real one. As long as I wipe off my prints, it'll be perfect."

Jesus seemed satisfied.

"When will we split up the money?" I asked.

"I don't want money. What would I do with it? I'm desperate, Neil. This is maybe the last opportunity for people to figure out the gravity of the situation. I'm back. I'm here to save the souls of those worthy of salvation. People seem to watch lots of television. Maybe they'll see me on TV. Maybe this could get the ball rolling."

"Why do you need me?" I asked.

"I can't explain that to you yet, Neil. It'll make sense later. Just trust me, and don't forget to bring the pellet gun in the morning."

NEIL 1:4

ON THE EVENING BEFORE THE ROBBERY I made a list of things I needed to do. After I'd accomplished every task, I planned to eat the list because I'd seen on television how masterminds had pulled off the perfect crime only to get caught with a to-do list.

I picked up Gina from soccer practice and hoped she wouldn't realize we were taking the longest route possible back home.

"Where we going?" she noticed.

"I just need to run in a store real fast?"

"What kinda store?"

"Just a store," I said.

"Probably a golf store. Mama says I can't get new cleats like Jenny Adamson because you spent the money on golf balls and a stupid glove."

"Your mother's a raving lunatic," I blurted out. "Besides, how many days in your twelve years of life have you gone without eating? How many nights have you slept outside in the rain? Or had no insurance, or cable TV, or Internet, or a refrigerator full of honey mustard?"

My voice rose through the sentence ending on a pitiful note. We were way beyond reason.

"What does honey mustard have to do with anything? I just don't understand why Jenny's dad can get her the cleats, but I have to use these old ones. That's all."

We pulled up into the Goodwill parking area.

"Oh my God," Gina said. "I will not get used cleats. They have foot fungus."

I turned off the car. "Why do you assume everything is for you? Maybe there's something I need."

"I'm not going inside," she said.

"Good. I'll leave the keys in the car. Maybe somebody'll kidnap you."

As I closed the door I heard her say, "Maybe they'll buy me some new cleats."

There were only two or three people in the store. I efficiently selected a camouflage fishing cap, a pair of dark-lens glasses, and a large flannel shirt, grey and green.

I stopped halfway between the front door of the store and my car. I could see Gina, her sock feet up on the dashboard, the sound of music inside vibrating.

There was still time to stop this craziness. Robbing a bank with Jesus, real or unreal, what could I hope to accomplish? All the money in the world wouldn't make Amanda, Elise, or Gina any happier. Within days they'd be back to complaining about the things they didn't have. Instead of cleats, it would be a certain car. Instead of a prom dress, it would be a new nose, higher cheek bones, a bigger diamond, a world without anxiety.

But I was gonna do it anyway, and I knew it, and I suppose Jesus knew it too. It was probably one of the reasons I was chosen. Maybe the only reason. I'd never been chosen before, for anything ever.

The next morning I must have driven around the grocery store parking lot ten times before I found a place I liked. I changed clothes in the front seat, adjusting my glasses and tilting the brim of the cap downward, tucking as much hair as possible into the edges of the hat. I stuffed a small pillow into the belly of the flannel shirt, adjusting it accordingly to make me look twenty pounds heavier. The pellet gun rested inside behind the pillow against my undershirt.

I tried to minimize the number of swings through the Wal-Mart parking lot and managed to locate a secluded spot on the third pass. Jesus was waiting for me in the wooded area between the back of Wal-Mart and Crescent Bank, just as he said he would.

"Good morning," he said. "Excellent disguise. You look like a guy I met in Kentucky."

"Are you sure about this thing?" I said.

"Yep. You go in the bank and get in line. Remember, I'll come in behind you in a few minutes, wave the gun around and have the teller fill a bag with money. I'll order you to bring me the bag and act like you'll be my hostage. Instead, run past me and out the door. I'll act surprised and keep everybody inside until you can get away. That's it."

"What if we end up in a gun battle?"

"A what?"

"A gun battle."

"I guess you better run faster. Are you a fast runner?"

"Not really."

We stood in the woods together. It was a pretty day, cool but not cold. I took the pellet gun from next to my stomach and wiped off the prints before handing it to Jesus.

"Okay, time to go," he said.

So I went. The parking lot in front of the bank had only a few cars. There was a red truck in the drive-thru window. When I opened the front door I was immediately struck by the total lack of customers. There were none. Two tellers eyeballed me across the empty lobby.

We hadn't planned for no customers. The security guard, a dark-skinned man in his sixties with a revolver on his hip, nodded his head like we were old friends. I nodded back, felt a wave of panic, and then spotted the chest-high table with deposit slips and pens. I pretended to fill out a deposit slip, listening for the sound of the door to open behind my back.

For some reason, and I'll never know why, I wrote the name of Nick Blankenship on the deposit slip. He was a guy I hated from high school and hadn't laid eyes on since we graduated. Seeing his name on the paper put me in strange state of mind, and I shuffled slowly toward the teller. She was a mousy girl, with one eye slightly higher than the other and a shiny face. We looked at each other, and I was sure she somehow knew the dark glasses weren't mine, and probably once belonged to a boat captain.

I began to slide the useless deposit slip across the smooth granite surface preparing for the odd conversation that would certainly follow and the possibility this Jesus fellow had simply stolen my pellet gun. The paper reached her thin dry fingers, but I held the edge tightly against the granite as she made a first attempt, and then a second, to take the deposit slip from me. It was then I heard the noise behind and turned to look over my left shoulder.

There he was, standing in the doorway, the pellet gun held above his head. We all froze.

"This is a robbery. Put your arms in the air. I'm holding a gun in my hand. You," he said, and pointed the gun at the mousy teller, "put all the money in a bag. Only the money. No dye packs or tracking devices."

I turned to the teller. She looked strangely calm and began putting handfuls of bills in a small canvas bank bag.

I glanced in the direction of the security guard. He seemed to be studying Jesus very closely, keeping both hands just above his head.

"You there," Jesus said, speaking to me. "Bring the bag over here. You'll be my hostage."

I took the bag from the teller and shuffled slowly toward the door.

The security guard said, "That ain't no real gun. That's a pellet gun."

We all looked at the gun at the same time. I ran out the door, turned the corner of the building, and hit the woods. I threw the small pillow into the bushes and replaced it with the bag of money so I wouldn't have to carry the thing. It was my own idea, and a good one I must say. No witnesses could testify later they saw a guy with a camouflage hat and flannel shirt carrying a bank bag.

I got to my car in the secluded Wal-Mart spot and drove slowly to the grocery store down the road. I parked in the place I selected earlier, changed clothes, and then threw the clothes, glasses, and hat into the Dumpster. I drove home and put the money in the toolshed waiting for darkness.

That night, when everyone was asleep, I hid the money in the corner of my toolshed instead of burying it in the yard like Jesus suggested. I just didn't want to take a chance of being double-crossed. You never know.

The next day on the Internet I saw the video from the bank security camera and learned what happened after I ran out the door.

They stood there all looking at each other for maybe

ten long seconds. Then Jesus said to the security guard, "How can you tell it's just a pellet gun?"

"Because it don't look like a real gun."

The sound of police sirens could be heard.

"And you ain't Jesus neither," the old man said.

"Why do you say that?"

"Because Jesus wouldn't rob a bank, and if he did, he sure wouldn't use no pellet gun."

EDWIN 1:1

THE DAY JESUS ROBBED THE BANK was twenty years to the day since I became the police chief of our fair little city. I'd been thinking about retirement, doing some fishing, maybe watching more baseball games. I've always loved fishing and baseball. They have a lot in common.

Curtis stuck his head in my office. "Chief, somebody just robbed the Crescent Bank. They said he's dressed like Jesus."

"Who's dressed like Jesus?"

"The bank robber."

"You gotta be kidding me."

"That's what they say," Curtis added.

Before I could put on my jacket and get out the door, Curtis stuck his head back in.

"Chief, line one, it's that lady from channel 5."

"How in the hell do those people find out things before they happen?"

Curtis said, "They hire some guy to sit around all day and listen to our radio calls."

I picked up the phone. "Linda, I don't have a comment yet. I haven't even gotten down to the bank to see what's going on."

Linda asked, "Have you ever heard of the Jesus Bandit before?"

"No," I said. "Have you?"

"No," she answered. "I just gave him the name. Remember where you heard it first."

I hung up the phone. The door to my office opened again and Frank Perry walked in, one of my newest investigators. He was all fired up, talking too fast, moving his hands around.

"Here's the story," he started. "This guy dressed like Jesus walks into the bank and stands at the door. He announces it's a robbery and holds a gun up over his head. He tells Becky, the teller—you know, the one with the weird eye—to put all the money in a bag. He tells her to hand it to this guy who's a customer in line, and then tells the guy to bring it to him. Instead, the customer runs out the bank and leaves Jesus standing at the door."

"Have we found this customer?" I asked.

"Not yet," he answered. "Anyway, the security guard gets to looking at the gun and realizes it's only a pellet pistol. A teller calls 911 and the guy just stands there until we get to the bank."

"Where is he?" I asked.

"They're bringing him in the back to the interrogation room right now. He looks exactly like those portraits of Jesus. Dressed just like him and everything. It's weird."

"Has he given a statement?" I asked.

"No. He says he'll only talk to you. He asked for you by name."

"Well," I said, "it's nice to hear Jesus knows my name. I feel a little better about dying."

Frank didn't smile. Curtis stuck his head back in the door.

"Chief, line two, it's some guy who says he's with the *New York Times*."

"Jesus Christ," I said. "Now you tell me how the goddamned *New York Times* hears about this story in fifteen minutes. Jesus must have decided to rob his first bank on the slowest news day in the history of the world."

Frank left in a hurry. I picked up the phone. "Chief Bastrop," I announced.

"Chief, this is Chris Young from the *New York Times*. I hear you got the Jesus Bandit in custody."

"Who told you that?" I asked.

"I got a call from one of our guys at the local paper down there. Just sounds like an interesting story."

"Mr. Young, I don't know anything yet. I haven't even been able to get out from behind my desk to find out what the hell is going on."

"Is there more than one person involved?" he asked.

"I told you I don't know anything yet. I'll talk to you when I do."

I hung up the phone and sat quietly in my office for a few seconds, just enjoying the silence, because I knew it would be hard to come by for a while.

EDWIN 1:2

OUR INTERROGATION ROOM IS TEN BY ten. Frank Perry guarded the door like Hitler was in custody.

He said, "I ran his prints, Chief. There's nothing."

"Nothing," I repeated. "Did he have any ID?"

"No," he said, stern-faced.

"Well, Frank, maybe it's really Jesus you've got locked up in that room, came back to save your soul, and you just don't recognize him."

Frank said, "That isn't funny, Chief. Jesus wouldn't rob a bank, and as a Christian, I would recognize my Savior."

I started to say, "Maybe you don't recognize him because you're not on the list," but it didn't seem necessary, so I just opened the door to the interrogation room and went inside alone.

Jesus sat at the table. There was a strange odor in the room, musty and ancient, like you might expect in one of those tombs in Egypt underneath a pyramid.

"Good morning," I said.

"Good morning," he repeated, and we shook hands like men.

"This has been an interesting morning," I said.

"Yes sir, it has," Jesus said.

I sat down across from him in the room. "My name is Edwin Bastrop. I'm the police chief. At least that's what it says on that little nameplate on my desk. Let's start out with a proper introduction. What's your name?"

He didn't really smile.

"You know my name, Chief. I don't want to get too personal. We both know there have been times in your life when your faith has been shaken, but you still know my name, and I still know yours."

He certainly looked the part. I've always been fascinated by the connection between mental illness and religion. After thirty-five years on the job, I've dealt with more crazy folks than I care to remember. In America, our mentally ill end up in two places: the emergency room and the courtroom. They end up with me one way or the other, and it seems a good number of them quote Bible verses or scream about the end of the world.

"If you're Jesus, why would you rob a bank? Thou shall not steal."

"I tried everything else. I tried preaching on street corners. I tried talking to priests and preachers at their churches. I've tried everything I know, but nobody paid any attention. I got arrested. I got committed. I got assaulted. And by the way, I didn't steal anything."

I said, "Well, somebody got away with $2,781.00 dollars. You wouldn't happen to know where I can find it, would you?"

"No," he answered, "but it's not really important."

"Who is Nick Blankenship?"

"I don't know," he answered. "Why?"

"That's the name on the deposit slip left at the bank by the guy that took off with the money."

"I don't know Mr. Blankenship, but I can assure you he had nothing whatsoever to do with the robbery of the bank."

I stopped. "Did somebody already read you your rights?"

"Yes, your assistant, Mr. Perry. I think he's mad at me."

I said, "He thinks you're mocking his Lord and Savior. You must get that a lot."

"Yes. Do you have any suggestions on how I can convince people I am who I am?"

"Not right now, I don't. We ran your fingerprints through the system and didn't get a hit. Do you mind if we take a little DNA sample? There's a separate database."

"You can take anything you want."

We looked at each other for a while. We just sat there, without speaking, and looked at each other. I don't think either one of us was the least bit uncomfortable with the silence.

Finally, Jesus said, "Now what?"

I waited a moment and responded to him, "I'm not really sure."

EDWIN 1:3

FRANK PERRY HAD THE TELLER, BECKY, sitting in his office waiting for me. She wasn't long out of high school. My mother would have said she had an unfortunate face. It was like a rodent. Not a bad rodent, but maybe like one of those small white mice.

"Chief, this is Becky Sullivan. She's the teller approached by the customer who ended up with the money," Frank Perry said.

"Hello, Becky."

"Hello, Chief. I recognize you from the drive-thru. You come on Friday mornings and drive a dark blue pickup truck."

It was hard to look at the girl when she spoke. One of her eyes was noticeably higher than the other, creating the illusion that she was two separate people.

"Did you recognize the customer who approached you?"

"No, I think he was using a disguise, but I recognized Jesus. He looks just like the picture in the recreation room at my church. Just like it."

"Did the customer say anything to you?"

"No. He wouldn't let go of the deposit slip. He slid it over to me, and when I tried to take it, the man just held it tight like he didn't really want me to have it in the first place."

Frank Perry said, "The name on the slip was Nick Blankenship. We checked. Nobody named Nick Blankenship has an account at the bank, but there is a guy in town with that name. I sent Curtis to go pick him up and bring him in for a few questions."

"Where's Jesus?" Becky said.

I started to tell her it wasn't really Jesus but there didn't seem to be a point. "He's in the back room."

"Is He under arrest? she asked.

"He robbed a bank. Yes, he is under arrest."

"When He came into the bank, there was peace that came over me. I knew he wouldn't hurt anybody."

She believed it was really Jesus who robbed her with a pellet gun a few hours earlier.

"Becky, I'm a man of facts. Unless he proves to me

that he's Jesus Christ—he's under arrest, and maybe even then."

She said, "He doesn't have to prove He's Jesus. Jesus doesn't have to prove anything to anybody. Somebody else has to prove He isn't, and until they do, I know what I know. There was peace in the bank when He came in the door. I could feel it like nothing I've ever felt before."

Becky's lower eye wandered slightly from our stare. She was a true believer, and it didn't matter much what I had to say. I had no desire to change her mind.

"Do you think, Becky, that the customer who gave you the deposit slip was in on the robbery?"

"His glasses didn't look right on him. They looked like a boat captain's glasses, not the type of glasses a person would wear in a bank on a regular day."

"What else did you notice?"

"He seemed to already be scared before Jesus came in the door."

"Anything else?" I asked.

"That's about all. Oh, he was wearing a wedding ring. I noticed it when he wouldn't let go of the deposit slip. It was silver with, like, tiny black braids around the edges on both sides. You know what I mean?"

"Could you draw it for me? Could you also give

a written statement with everything you can remember?"

She tilted her head to the side slightly. "I'm not gonna do anything to help you put Jesus in jail."

I didn't want to draw a line in the sand with her. She waited for my response.

"Okay," I said.

Becky smiled, and then started to sketch a wedding ring in elaborate detail, her pen moving swiftly and deliberately across the white page. She had genuine talent, an eye for the details, and a God-given ability to sketch such details for others to see. I was impressed.

EDWIN 1:4

I SAT AT MY DESK WITH Frank sitting across from me. He was even more uncomfortable than usual, his hands fidgeting in his lap.

"I know it's not true and all," he said, "but what if it's really Jesus sitting in our interrogation room? What if he came back like everyone thought he would, but the world has changed so much nobody will give him the time of day?"

I let him think a moment about what he'd said. "Frank, don't be stupid. It's just another crazy son-of-a-bitch with a chemical imbalance who happened to end up in our damn town instead of a town down the road."

"I'm just sayin', what if?"

"We don't deal in what ifs. We deal in facts. We deal

in law. We're police officers. Now, who else you got for us to talk to?"

 Frank looked down at his notepad.

"Nick Blankenship. He's a car salesman up at the Ford place. It wasn't him at the bank this morning, though. He got to work early and was there all day. He's an asshole."

"Excellent. That's just what we need in this circus. An asshole."

We walked down the hall to Curtis's office where Mr. Blankenship waited.

"Great," Nick Blankenship said. "Maybe somebody has shown up who can tell me why the hell I got dragged down here."

"Do you know anybody at the Crescent Bank?" I asked.

"No."

"Do you know of any reason your name would be written on a deposit slip handed to a bank teller this morning during a robbery?"

"Hell no. Is this about the Jesus Bandit? I heard about that shit on the radio. Somebody oughta take that punk around the back of the station and kick his fake-Jesus ass."

"Thank you for coming down, Mr. Blankenship.

You can go back to your car lot."

He was indignant. "Is that all you've got to say? You drag my ass down here in the middle of a sale I was about to close, ask me two questions, and I'm excused? That's all you've got to say?"

I took a deep breath. "In my opinion, Mr. Blankenship, mankind will go the way of the honeybee, kind of a symbolic canary in a coalmine. We've poisoned our bees, the creatures responsible for pollination of our food supply."

Nick Blankenship squinted his eyes at me.

"What a buncha bullshit," he said, and slammed the door on his way out.

I walked down the hall to the interrogation room, where Jesus sat drinking a cold Coke. I brought Frank with me, and we all three sat at the table.

I said, "We found a small pillow in the woods behind the bank. Is it yours?"

"No," he said.

"I think you're telling the truth about Mr. Blankenship not being involved, but I haven't figured out why his name was on the deposit slip. Maybe it was just a made-up name and it's a coincidence that there happens to be a guy in town with the same name."

"Is this going to be on TV?"

"Is what going to be on TV?"

"All this about the robbery at the bank? My picture? Will it be on the television?"

"Do you want it to be?" I asked.

"Yes. It seems to be the only way for people to find out I'm here. If not, it was all for nothing."

"I'll tell you what." I said, "If you'll tell me about this other guy who helped you this morning, I'll think about letting the TV cameras get a look at you."

He looked down at his Coke. "I told you, Mr. Blankenship had nothing to do with this."

"Well, I think the customer in the bank who ended up with the money was working with you, and whatever went wrong, he ended up with the money and left you high and dry. If you can help me get him, and get the money back, things could go a lot better for you."

He turned from me and stared toward the door. I thought for a moment the man might cry, and he seemed to think deeply about what I'd said. Becky was right. He looked exactly like the portrait of Jesus we've all seen before, staring off into some Heavenly distance.

Finally he said, "In the place where the tree falleth, there it shall be."

I waited. "I'm not sure what that means."

Jesus said, "I'd like to go to sleep now."

EDWIN 1:5

BY AFTERNOON IT WAS ALL OVER the television. The phone was ringing off the hook. Apparently, the Internet news stations picked up the story of the "Jesus Bandit" and it went from one end of the Earth to the other in a matter of seconds. Somehow the video from the bank security cameras was leaked or hacked or whatever the hell you call it. The image of Jesus standing with a pellet pistol over his head was big-time news, all over the Internet.

At home that evening I turned off or unplugged every phone in the house and lay in bed next to my wife with the TV off. She was accustomed to giving me a certain amount of space to unwind from my job.

"What's he like?" she asked, as she turned the page of her *People* magazine.

"Who?" I said, pretending not to know.

We'd been together for a very long time. She knew I knew who she was talking about, so she waited patiently.

I said, "After he was put in the holding cell, I watched him from a spot he couldn't see me."

"Why?" she asked.

"That's the question I asked myself. I guess maybe I expected to see him do something when he thought he was alone he might not do if he really was Jesus. I guess I thought I'd be able to jump out of my hiding place and yell 'Aha.'"

"What did he do?" she asked.

"He just laid there."

"He didn't have anything in his pockets?" she asked. "No identification, no credit cards, no money?"

"He didn't have any pockets."

We were quiet for a time. The page of the magazine turned.

"I feel sorry for his family," she said. "They must be wondering where he is, what happened to him."

"I'm gonna hook him up to the polygraph machine tomorrow, and I'll bet you ten dollars he passes. I'll bet you my last ten dollars this guy believes he's Jesus to the point he'll fool the polygraph."

"With all this publicity, maybe somebody will recognize him and you'll get a call tomorrow that clears all this up."

I could feel sleep pulling me down. The energy left my body.

"When this is over, I think I'll go fishin'," is the last thing I remember saying. Maybe I never said it at all. Maybe it was just a thought that never made it out into the world.

I dreamed the sky turned black and rotten. It was worse than any rolling storm I'd ever seen, the blackness boiling over and falling downward until I couldn't see an inch in front of my face. It was like smoke but without heat or odor, and kept coming and coming until everything was dead.

EDWIN 1:6

THE NEXT MORNING, WHEN I ARRIVED at the office, a man waited for me in the lobby.

He stuck out his hand, "I'm Chris Young. We talked on the phone yesterday."

"Yeah, you're from the *New York Times*. It's a long way to come for a pellet gun robbery."

"A what?" he asked.

"A pellet gun robbery. That's what he used to rob the bank. A pellet gun."

"I don't care about that, Chief. Have you been able to figure out who this guy is?"

"No," I said, as he followed me into my office.

"No fingerprint match?"

"No."

"No calls from all this publicity?"

"No."

"Any tattoos?"

"No."

"Any specific accent?"

"Not really."

"Nothing in his clothes, receipts, documents, anything?"

"Nothing."

"Who do you think the guy is?"

"Well, Becky Sullivan thinks he's Jesus."

"Who's Becky Sullivan?"

"The teller at the bank."

"What proof does she base that on?"

"The peaceful feeling she got when he entered the bank and demanded the money."

All along he was recording our conversation, but I didn't care. What's the difference?

"She's going to have to do better than that. I'll need a bit more than a peaceful feeling to be convinced that Jesus is sitting in your jail."

I looked at the man for the first time. Mid-thirties. Black man. Educated. New York accent. He wore a lightweight blue sweater and hadn't shaved in at least a few days.

"Do you believe in God, Mr. Young?"

"No, Chief, I don't."

"Did you come all this way to prove the believers wrong?"

"No, I came all this way because it's a good story, and it sells papers. It's an even better story if he's really Jesus."

"I suppose it is," I said, and turned to look out my only window. It was cloudy outside, a little cooler than yesterday. The fishing would be good, I thought.

"Can I see him?" the reporter asked.

I'd almost forgotten that he was still in the room.

"If he wants to see you, Mr. Young, you can see him, but you have to make one promise."

"What's that?"

"You have to promise to be nice to him."

There was hesitation. "I don't understand."

"Who says you have to understand everything, Mr. Young? Just make me the promise, and if he wants to see you after the polygraph test, you can meet with him."

He looked at me for an explanation, but I didn't have one.

"I promise," he finally said, but I knew I couldn't be sure he wasn't a liar.

CHRIS 1:1

CHIEF BASTROP LEFT ME ALONE IN his office. It was sparse, almost like he expected to leave the place any minute and never return. There was one framed picture on the shelf, the chief with a woman I assumed was his wife, both smiling, probably taken ten years earlier. There was a lake in the background.

I started to wonder why I'd volunteered to cover this story in person instead of with phone calls and e-mails. There was just something about the guy, dressed like Jesus, standing at the doorway of the bank holding a pistol. I'd watched the video over and over. He moved slowly and spoke quietly, without anger or hostility, the way we've been programmed to believe Jesus might move and speak.

Someone would argue this stereotypical behavior was definitive evidence the man wasn't Jesus at all. Someone like Becky Sullivan might say the same behavior was definitive proof the man was indeed the Son of God. I just couldn't get the visual image out of my head of Jesus robbing a bank, clearly wishing to get caught, with that stupid pellet gun over his head.

The chief came back in the office and said, "He says he'll talk to you. The polygraph will take a few hours. Why don't you come back after lunch?"

I asked, "When he's hooked up to this lie detector test, are you going to ask him questions about his identity, or just ask questions about the bank robbery?"

"Both," he answered.

"Will you provide to me a list of the questions and the results?"

The chief sat down in his chair. I noticed he glanced at the photograph of him and his wife.

"I'm not sure about that," he said. "As we both know, polygraphs aren't admissible in court. I expect somebody up in the DA's office is gonna get in the middle of this soon enough and start telling me what to do."

He glanced back at his photograph. "You married?" he asked.

"No," I said. "Almost, once, but I couldn't pull the trigger. You?"

"Yeah," he said.

"Any kids?" I asked.

He hesitated just slightly. "No," he said, but it was much more than that. There was something underneath the answer. He'd lost a child, or wanted one but wasn't able. His eyes gave it away.

"Do you believe in God?" the chief asked me again.

"No, Chief, I don't. I believe in what I can see, and taste, and feel, and hear, and smell."

"How old are you?" he asked.

"Thirty-three."

Chief Bastrop leaned back in his chair.

"Thirty-three?" he repeated.

"Yes."

He said, "That's the same age Jesus was when he died. Thirty-three. Do you think that's a coincidence?"

"Yes, I do."

He looked tired. Not just tired from a bad night's sleep, but weary from years of wearing down, kind of like an old set of tires, no tread left but still functional.

He said, "They did this experiment where they asked a group of people to answer a certain question. The purpose of the question was to separate people based on whether they were more intuitive or more reflective in their reasoning.

"It turns out that people who are more intuitive are much more likely to believe in God, a higher power, and the ones that are more reflective, rational, are less likely to believe."

"What was the question?" I asked.

Chief Bastrop looked at me like he was trying to remember the exact words of the question.

Finally, he said, "A bat and a ball cost a total of $1.10. The bat costs $1.00 more than the ball. How much does the ball cost?"

I wanted to answer quickly, probably to show how smart I was, but after being told the purpose of the question, I took an extra few seconds to run the numbers in my head.

"Five cents," I said.

He smiled, and I wondered whether he detected the extra seconds I took to respond. Would I have answered differently without the prelude?

"Well, I guess that makes you a non-believer. An intuitive person says ten cents, because their first impulse is to knock off $1.00 from the total. The person who relies on reasoning is more likely to go beyond the first impulse and find the correct answer."

I asked him, "Do you believe in God, Chief?"

He looked me in the eye. "Yeah, I do."

"Why?" I asked.

He said, "Because I won't settle for anything less. That's it."

CHRIS 1:2

I NSTEAD OF WASTING THE MORNING, I decided to meet with Becky Sullivan. She wasn't hard to find, and we sat down at a local restaurant across from each other in a booth.

"Have you seen Him yet, in person?" she asked.

"Not yet. I'll probably talk to him this afternoon."

"You'll see."

"See what?"

"You'll see. It's not really His looks, it's how He makes you feel."

"And how is that?"

She was very animated. Her small hands danced in front of us, emphasizing, demanding attention. She had this wandering eye that was disconcerting, but her hands seemed to compensate for any lack of connection.

"The only way I can describe it," she said, "is to say it's like this feeling comes over you. A warm feeling. Maybe like it would feel if we could remember being in the womb. Except better, because there's this certainty, this knowing everything will be alright. It's like He lifts a weight off you. The weight of just living. I don't know how else to say it."

"I watched the video from the bank camera. Do you know how it got released so fast?"

Becky answered too quickly. "No."

"Did you do it, Becky? Maybe so the world could see this man that you think is Jesus? Maybe to help?"

She said strongly, "People need to know. People need to know Jesus has come back."

She poured a tremendous amount of sugar in her coffee and stirred furiously, the spoon tinking against the side of the white porcelain cup.

"When did you talk to the police?" I asked.

"Yesterday. They asked me lots of questions about the other man. The man who ran off with the money. But I don't really care whether he was involved or not."

"Have you thought of anything about the other man that you didn't tell the police? Anything new you remembered? His clothes, his face, cologne, anything at all?"

"I told them about his wedding ring, and how he didn't want to let go of the deposit slip, and how he seemed real nervous before Jesus even came in the bank. They said the name on the slip, Nick Blankenship, wasn't his real name. I heard Mr. Blankenship works up at the car dealership by the interstate."

She changed the subject. "We're gonna get Him out on bond. We're already raising the money. Lots of people, some from far off, are helping. If we can get Him out He can stay in my basement free. I know a lawyer who says he'll help us out. He's not really a criminal lawyer. I think he does wills and stuff, but he says that he'll help us out."

I took a sip of my coffee. "What if he doesn't want to stay in your basement?"

"What do you mean?" she said. Her face tightened up. She resembled a badger.

"What if he doesn't want to stay in your basement? What if he'd rather stay in a nice motel, with a pool, and a breakfast buffet downstairs?"

I smiled just a little bit, both because I liked picturing Jesus at a breakfast buffet, and also because I didn't want Becky to stop talking to me.

"Oh, I get it. You're just playin'. I wonder what He likes for breakfast. Do you think He likes sausage?"

"Everybody likes sausage," I said, and then gently steered the conversation back where it belonged.

"Have you thought of anything else about the other man?"

"Yes," she said. "When I told my husband about everything last night, I remembered the man was wearing a shirt that looked exactly like the shirt my husband had. It was heavy, flannel, kinda greenish lumberjack shirt. I remembered it because my husband wore it all the time. I finally gave it away to the Goodwill store up on Jacoby Street. Took a load of old clothes and stuff."

"What color was it exactly?"

"Kind of green and grey. The man wore it over another shirt underneath. It looked exactly like my husband's old shirt. It even had a tear in the pocket the same place. I remember telling my husband he couldn't wear that shirt to church anymore. It was ugly anyway. I hated it."

"How long ago did you take it to the Goodwill?"

"About two weeks ago, I guess. I got a receipt somewhere. For taxes, you know."

She actually got quiet a moment, staring into her coffee. Then she whispered to herself, "I hated that shirt."

CHRIS 1:3

THE CHIEF WAS STANDING IN THE lobby of the police department talking to an officer when I entered after lunch. He saw me coming before I opened the glass door.

"How'd the polygraph test go?" I asked.

"How did it go?" he repeated. "I guess that depends on where you stand. He admitted robbing the bank, believes without question he's Jesus Christ, and he'd rather talk to you than a lawyer."

"Good, because I'm ready to talk to him, too. I hear the true believers are raising bond money, and he might be harder to corner once he's out."

The deputy patted me down and walked me through a metal detector. I was led to a small room with only a table and two chairs. In one of the chairs sat the man

I'd seen on the bank surveillance camera holding a gun over his head. I was immediately struck by how remarkably the man looked like we think Jesus should look.

His beard wasn't well manicured, but I wouldn't say it was scraggly either. There was a smell, like an old house, or a trunk in an attic. Musty, but not altogether unpleasant.

"My name is Chris Young. I'm with the *New York Times*."

We shook hands.

"I appreciate you seeing me," I said.

"No, I'm the one who's appreciative."

"It's not often Jesus robs a bank."

"I hope not," he said. "In times of desperation, I suppose we will do desperate things."

"Did you need money?" I asked.

"Of course not."

I waited for him to elaborate, and placed my tape recorder on the table in front of us.

"I expected resistance," he said, in a soft voice, "but I didn't expect indifference. I knew it wouldn't be easy, but truthfully, I wasn't prepared for how different the world has become in only a few thousand years. One of the limitations of coming back in the human form is leaving behind perfect knowledge."

"How's it changed?" I asked.

"I've traveled, but the people in all the places that I visited seemed too busy, too preoccupied, to take the time to recognize the significance of who I am, and the message I carry."

"How long have you been back?" I asked, paying very close attention to the man's voice and face. He seemed to have no particular expression. Not blank, but maybe above the words. A higher concern.

"Months," he said. "I couldn't give up. That's why I did what I did. People spend so much time staring at their devices. Televisions, computers, phones. I figured my best chance was to come to them through these devices, and from what I can tell, nobody pays much attention to anything without shock value."

He was very calm and focused, which aren't generally characteristics of the mentally ill. There was no obvious financial agenda.

"They call you the 'Jesus Bandit,'" I said. "What do you think of that?"

He smiled. There were long lines in his face. Lines that revealed a man who has smiled before. It was very natural on him.

"Yes," he simply said.

"Did you have an accomplice?" I asked.

The smile faded slowly away. He seemed disappointed that I asked such a question.

"Nick Blankenship?" I said, hoping for a reaction.

The man waited a significant amount of time, and then said slowly, "The sluggard is wiser in his own conceit than seven men that can render a reason."

We both waited.

I said, "Anybody can quote the Bible and dress up like Jesus. I don't believe in God, and I don't believe you're the Son of God."

I was surprised at the stern delivery of my words. So I leaned back gently in my chair to counter the possible perceived aggression.

"I know, Chris. That's why I asked to see you. The window is closing. I'll only be a worthwhile story for a few days. No one out there will pay attention to the true believers, the zealots shoving me down people's throats. My presence must be announced by the doubters, mocked by the non-believers, crucified, if you will, by the educated and powerful.

"You're the man for the job, Chris Young. We can use each other to accomplish our separate goals."

His voice held no urgency or desire to sell himself. I felt strangely out of control.

"I'm gonna figure out who you are."

He looked at me for a long moment. Neither of us blinked or smiled.

"I hope you do," he said. And he seemed like he genuinely meant it.

"People are raising bond money to get you out. They're finding you a lawyer, and a place to stay. I hope you don't mind sleeping in a basement."

"I've slept in far worse places, Mr. Young. Far worse than a basement. I hope that we can meet again tomorrow. I need some time to think about things and rest."

"Can I take your picture?" I asked.

At the time, I had no idea how important this last-minute picture would be. It was really just an afterthought.

"Okay," he said, and closed his eyes. He put his hands together in front of him on the table, one over the other, and then titled his head down, eyes still closed. I angled the shot to capture the cream-colored cinderblock background of the jail setting, and later, when the picture was printed, there was the strangest muted yellow light in the room around him. A light I hadn't noticed as we spoke that day.

CHRIS 1:4

LEAVING THE POLICE STATION, I SAW the chief down the hall. He was talking to a man I didn't recognize, and the chief left the man and headed in my direction deliberately.

He said, "Do you have any idea how many calls and e-mails we've received from the media people? I got a call a few minutes ago from China. Goddamned China."

"It'll be worse tomorrow."

"Why?" he asked sternly.

"Because my piece will be in tomorrow's *Times*, and once that hits, anyone who hasn't already heard of the Jesus Bandit will jump on the runaway train."

He took a long breath, and his tired eyes drifted to a window.

"Don't worry," I said. "It won't last long."

He didn't look at me. "What do you mean?"

"The story. They never last very long. There will be another one in a few days. And then another. Somebody'll blow something up, or kidnap a child, or beat a dictator bloody in the streets. This Jesus guy won't last too long."

He put his hands in his jacket pockets. "I guess my definition of too long might be different from yours. After you leave, and go cover the next big thing, I'll still be here. The stories you leave behind don't just go away for the people in the middle of them."

He had a point. I noticed recently how I cared less and less about the people I met. Maybe it was just good journalism to remove myself from old stories so I could commit to new ones. Or maybe it was self-preservation. A man can only see so many corpses before he loses reverence.

"Maybe so," I said.

"What do you think of our bank robber?"

"Until we know who he is, it's all a big mystery. It's easy to be mysterious when you're not burdened by all the petty little facts of the past. Like criminal records, failed marriages, IRS debts."

"So you don't think he's Jesus?"

"No, I don't, and I hope you don't either. He wants to talk with me again tomorrow."

A lady's voice behind me said, "Chief, line three."

The chief said sarcastically, "Is it China?"

The lady hesitated, and said meekly, "I don't think so. Sounded like Ed Baines."

The chief, as he walked away, said to me, "I've heard the same rumors you've heard. Some folks are trying to raise up the money to get our robber out on bond. I hope the son-of-a-bitch takes the first bus to Mexico."

Back at the hotel I got a call from my editor, Stanley Keenan.

" You gonna make deadline on this story?"

"Yeah. I'll have it to you in an hour. And by the way, I've got a pretty good photograph I hope you'll run."

"There's a new angle to this," he said.

"What's that?"

"There's a lady in California. Her name is Beth Anderson. She thinks this Jesus Bandit might be her son. There's a lot more to it, but she's flying to see you. Wants to talk to you and see Jesus in person. She'll be in the lobby of your hotel at nine in the morning. Beth Anderson."

"That'll be perfect," I said. "The first article can be all mysterious and quirky. The follow-up can solve the mystery with a human interest touch."

I FINISHED THE STORY AND SENT it to Stanley with the photograph. It was coming together nicely. If the man in jail was Beth Anderson's son, the next article, and the last as far as I was concerned, would show a picture of Ms. Anderson side by side with the booking photograph of her long-lost son. And then readers would get to hear the sad story of drugs, or mental illness, or physical abuse, or the Jesus Bandit's premeditated attempt to draw attention to his delusional world view.

I slept well and woke to the sound of a woman talking loudly on a telephone. "There's just no way I can go to that wedding," she said. "After what Lisa wrote about your sister, I don't see how you can go either."

The words were clear, almost like there was no wall between us, and certainly like this woman didn't know or didn't care there were other inhabitants in the hotel.

I showered and went downstairs to the lobby carrying my cup of coffee at ten minutes till nine.

The lobby of the hotel was fairly small. Mostly it consisted of a pinkish couch surrounded by two chairs and a coffee table. There was a muted big-screen television on a news channel.

I stopped a distance away and watched the lady sitting alone on the couch. She was white, mid-fifties, pleasant-looking, wearing a casual dark dress, and reading a folded newspaper. It was my paper, and she was reading my article.

I watched her extend the paper, squinting without her glasses to read the words, and then drawing the newspaper nearer in order to look more closely, I assumed, at the photograph of the man she believed to be her son.

Mostly, as I watched the woman, I felt sadness around her. She was a long way from home, sitting in a generic hotel lobby, waiting to meet a stranger. It was obvious the woman would never have come so far unless there was desperation, and for me, desperation always added a helpful element.

She set the paper down on the coffee table and closed her eyes slowly, just sitting alone on the couch, eyes closed, in her own private world. When the lady opened her eyes again, she looked directly at me, and for an instant I felt like a kid peeking through a bedroom window.

There was something about the way she looked at

me. Like she hoped that I would just stay where I stood and not come any closer, because whatever she learned from me, one way or the other, would be bad news, and the seconds between herself and the next bad news were ticking away.

BETH 1:1

I KNEW THE MAN LOOKING AT me from across the lobby was the reporter from the *New York Times*, but I couldn't make myself move. For what seemed like a long time, neither of us smiled or motioned.

I am a woman. I have been a daughter, a wife, and a mother, but those things can change. When my parents died I was no longer a daughter. When my husband finally filed for divorce, I was no longer a wife. And now I've come here to find out if I'm still a mother.

I kept thinking to myself, "This is a big mistake. I should have stayed at home."

And then I would think to myself, "But it might be him. It might be David."

Maybe it would have been better if I'd just stood up, walked out the front door, and gone home, but I didn't, and at some point one of us, and I can't remember who, changed facial expression and the spell was broken.

"I'm Chris Young," he said, and sat down in the chair to my left.

"Thank you for meeting me. I'm Beth Anderson."

"You've come a long way, Ms. Anderson."

"I have. I hope it wasn't a mistake."

"I'm told you think the man in jail here for the bank robbery might be your son."

"I saw his face on that videotape. It was grainy, I know, but there was just something that made me watch it again and again. Something about the eyes, I think."

"When's the last time you saw your son?" he asked.

I knew I would have to tell the whole story again. I'd gotten good through the years at leaving out certain parts. The repetition has become familiar and comfortable.

"It's been almost four years," I answered.

"How old is he?"

"Thirty-four."

Mr. Young jotted a few notes. I couldn't tell whether he felt I was a waste of his time, or whether he really wanted to hear the rest of my story.

"I know it must sound strange to you," I said. "A mother who thinks her son, gone for four years, might have dressed up like Jesus and robbed a bank."

I think he could see how fragile I was. I think he could tell any minute I might shatter like a crystal glass and end up in pieces on the floor beneath his feet. It's the way I felt, and I'm quite sure it's the way I looked.

"We couldn't have children," is how I started. "At least that's what the doctors told us. We tried one thing and then the other. After a time it all runs together. I think both of us reached a point where we were resigned to the idea it would never happen. And then, I got pregnant."

He didn't push me. Mr. Young let me tell the story at my own pace. I appreciated his patience. If I was capable of such a thing, I would have admitted to myself how much I needed to tell the story to whomever would listen.

"David was born. As perfect as anything God ever put on this Earth. It was truly a miracle after all those years of doctors telling us it couldn't happen.

"Everything was normal. He started talking early. He was out of diapers on time. Just a curious, interesting, affectionate, wonderful, wonderful, child."

I felt the tears come to my eyes like they'd come so

many times before. I wiped them away with the tip of my index finger and waited a moment for the emotion to pass.

"What happened?" he asked gently.

I took a deep breath.

"He was seven. At the ballpark. He loved baseball. He loved the hats, and the uniforms, and all the little baseball talk.

"I didn't actually see it happen, but in my mind sometimes I think I did.

"They said he bent down to pick up his glove. The other boy was swinging a bat. David stood up at the exact wrong second. Maybe one second earlier, or one second later, and he's just rubbing his shoulder, or maybe got a knot on his head. You know?

"But it wasn't just a knot on his head. He was in a coma for three days. We never left the hospital. They told us there was bleeding on his brain. They told us there was swelling.

"For three days he never opened his eyes."

It was like I was in the room with him again. It was like it was all happening again, but dulled by time, worn down by repetition, but alive for me again.

"They said he would die. Maybe it would have been better," I heard myself say, the words tailing away.

"Maybe it would have been better for everybody."

Mr. Young asked, "Did he suffer brain damage?"

I looked at the man in the chair next to me. He was about the same age as David, the brown skin on his face smooth around his eyes. I wondered about his parents.

"When he woke up," I said, "he was never the same person. It was like he was a completely different boy. Quiet, distant, just odd. It was like we were strangers to him. There were specialists, new medicines, but it was always the same.

"He would walk past our house on the way home from school, and we'd find him blocks away. He told me once that when he was asleep in the coma, God had come to him and said He would need to remove the soul of the old David, and replace it with a different soul.

"When he grew up, he changed his name to David Corn. We don't know why. He disappeared for months at a time, couldn't keep a job, self-medicated. It was like he was lost."

Chris Young said, "It must have been very hard."

"For us," I asked, "or for him?"

"Everybody, I guess."

"I never saw my little boy again after that day at

the baseball park. Not even a glimpse of him. Not one single moment. But you can't give up hope, you know? You can't give it up. I prayed he'd bump his head again and wake up who he used to be. What if some combination of medicine or bad drugs flip a switch in his brain, and now he's scared, that wonderful little boy, wondering where his mother and father are? He'd be afraid and alone, lonelier than God."

My entire body was empty of energy. I felt like dead weight, unable to move from my spot on the pink couch. Was it a mistake to come to this place? What's the opposite of a miracle?

Mr. Young said, "I'm going to see him at the police station in a few hours. Would you like to come with me?"

I thought about it for a moment and said, "I don't really have a choice, do I?"

Chris Young said, "We all have choices, Ms. Anderson, but I agree. I don't see how you could go home not knowing."

"I've gone a very long time not knowing, Mr. Young. A very long time."

BETH 1:2

I RODE WITH MR. YOUNG TO the police station. The day was mostly grey and cloudy. I wondered what the weather was like at home. There had been no conversation with my ex-husband about traveling with me to see the man we'd both seen on television.

"Oh, God," I'd said to him on the phone when they showed the grainy video of the bank robber.

"What?" Ken asked.

"It looks like David," I said.

I could picture my ex-husband closing his eyes and rubbing his face like I'd seen him do many times before. We had to be feeling all the same things about losing our son, but our reactions to the feelings couldn't have been further apart.

Ken gave up. I'm not sure when it happened exactly,

but he gave up. To survive, I think he needed to put it all away in a nice neat place, like inside a box in the attic. You know it's there, and you know you can open it anytime you want, but you never do. The box just stays sealed up in the attic. And days pass.

I think the only reason we stayed together as long as we did was because we knew how terrible it would be alone. We shared a sadness, and isn't it always better to share sadness than face it by yourself?

Chris Young interrupted my thoughts. "I've been thinking about how you'd like to first see the man you think might be your son. I don't know if they have one of those rooms with the two-way mirror."

"It's his voice," I said calmly. "I have to hear his voice. Through the years he's changed so much physically. Beards, extra weight, one time he even shaved his head, but he can't change his voice. I'll know it's him or not in just a few words."

We rode along in silence.

Mr. Young said curiously, "What if it's not him? What if it's not David?"

"Then I'll go home."

The light turned red and we came to a stop. I could feel the anxiety thickening in my chest as we left the light and got closer to where we were going. Closer to knowing.

"What if it is David?" he asked.

We were passing a school. There was a group of children, maybe fourth or fifth graders, playing in the field. One boy was off to the side alone. He sat next to a tree looking down at something in the grass. His hair was brown, and he never looked up from the spot in the grass as we passed by.

"I don't know, Mr. Young," was all I could think to say.

At the police station we waited in the lobby for the local chief of police. I liked his face. I don't know why. Maybe he reminded me of someone.

"Chief, this is Beth Anderson. Ms. Anderson, this is Chief Bastrop."

We shook hands. I could tell he wasn't expecting me.

"Ms. Anderson has come to see our bank robber. She thinks it might be her son. He suffered a head injury when he was a small boy, and since then he kind of wanders in and out of their lives."

"Mostly out," I said.

"I'm sorry," the chief said, and I believed he meant it. There was wisdom in his eyes. How many parents had he told through the years of their sons or daughters dying in car wrecks, or accidental shootings? How much bad news had he carried from one place to the other, dropping it off but still keeping a part of it with him? A lot, I would think.

"It's been four years since I've seen him," I said. "He was on TV, on that video, but I couldn't be sure. If I could just hear his voice, I think I'll know."

The chief hesitated. "Well, we haven't been able to come up with a single clue of who he is, so I suppose it won't hurt. We'll let Chris meet with him in a regular room, and we'll stand outside the door where we can hear."

We all moved toward a metal detector that I assumed led to the jail area.

Chris asked, "Have you made any headway figuring out who the accomplice might be?"

"No, not yet. We've enhanced his face from the surveillance video, but it's really poor quality. There were no prints. We'll figure it out."

The three of us ended up standing next to a large metal door in a hallway. A tall guard was at the door waiting for the chief to tell him what to do next.

Chief Bastrop said, "Chris, Ms. Anderson will stand out here by me where he can't see us. The guard, Anthony here, will stand at the crack in the door."

"I'll just get him talking," Chris said.

The chief said, "And don't forget to keep your promise, Chris."

The men looked at each other. The anxiety rose back into my chest. I would hear his voice soon. And they would look at me for an answer. What to pray for now? What's best?

The guard unlocked the heavy door and Chris went inside. I stood with my back against the cold cement wall and waited.

Chris's voice: "Good morning."

Another man's voice. Almost a whisper. Too quiet to hear.

Chris's voice: "Did you sleep well?"

"Yes."

Not enough to tell. I leaned my head closer to the crack in the door, straining to hear. I leaned too far, and as I turned my head, there he sits, ten feet away in the room at the table with Chris. He sees me. He looks exactly like Jesus. Exactly like the picture in my childhood Bible.

Chris turns to look at me. I feel the chief's hand on my arm, but he doesn't pull me back. He lets me stand in the opening. It's like it's happening all over again.

Chris finally speaks. "This is Ms. Anderson. She

believes you might be her son."

We looked at one another. The tightness in my chest began to loosen slowly. It seemed each breath came easier, and then easier.

It wasn't my son. It wasn't David. But for some reason, I didn't feel the disappointment I expected. There was no wave of sadness.

Instead, I can't describe the stillness I felt standing at the door of that room.

We were looking at each other. Still ten feet apart, when he said gently, "I'm sorry."

"You have nothing to be sorry for," I said, and turned slowly from the doorway until my back was against the wall again. I took a long, deep breath, and from inside the room, I heard the man's voice, the man who wasn't my son, say, "Sometimes it seems the covers of this book are too far apart."

I knew exactly what he meant.

BETH 1:3

SITTING QUIETLY IN THE CHIEF'S OFFICE, he said to me, "I'll drive you back to your hotel. I expect Chris will be a while."

On the bookshelf to my left, eye level, there was a photograph of Chief Bastrop and his wife. I didn't have to ask who she was. It was obvious they'd been together for a long time. She wasn't necessarily a pretty lady, and he wasn't a handsome man, but together they were something more. They were two sides of the same face.

"Do you have any children?" I asked, looking at the photograph.

He didn't answer quickly, but instead, seemed to think about the question a moment.

"No," he said.

I looked down at my thin hands folded neatly in

my lap. It was my favorite dress. Favorite because I'd worn it the day before David's accident so many years ago. It still fit. A little snug in the waist, but still just fine.

I HADN'T BEEN ABLE TO THROW it away. All those times we'd gone through the house getting together old clothes and things for Goodwill, and each time I left the dress hanging in my closet in the same place.

How could I give it away? How could I see another woman in the grocery store and wonder if it was the dress I'd worn with David that day we held hands in the park? His little hand was so tight in mine while we walked together and talked about why birds are different colors.

"Mom, I wish I was a bird. Not so I could fly away, but so I could always fly home."

I remember thinking that he wouldn't want to hold my hand much longer. Soon, he would be embarrassed to hold my hand walking in the park. I remember squeezing a little harder, and David squeezed just a little harder himself, almost like there was a part of him that knew. Knew what? Knew what would happen the next day? How could he know?

The chief said, "I'm sorry it wasn't your son."

He was genuine, but it didn't really matter.

I said, "If David had died that day at the ballpark, I sometimes wonder if I could have lived. If he had died in the hospital bed instead of waking up from the coma, I don't know if I could have lived another day, found any reason, any reason at all, to get out of bed in the morning and spend another day in a world where a little boy dies for no reason, no reason at all.

"It's almost like God knew that, so instead of taking David's body, he only took his soul and left his body here so there would be some hope for me. Some hope, like today, that David is out there, and he needs me. Do you see what I'm saying?"

"Yes," he said, "I do."

We sat quietly. There were noises outside the office door. Phones ringing. A door closing. A woman said, "I'll be glad when he's gone."

I said, "When I knew it wasn't David. When I knew it wasn't his voice, the first thing I felt was relief."

I looked into the chief's face. It was different than it had been earlier. Fuller, somehow. Almost like a different face than the one I'd seen when we first met just minutes earlier.

"Do you think that's wrong?" I asked.

Chief Bastrop's eyes traveled to the photograph of

him and his wife on the bookshelf. He had his own story, and it wasn't my story. It had nothing to do with me at all, and I could see him drifting to himself.

"I don't know, Ms. Anderson," he finally said.

We were quiet again. I felt the nausea of guilt for not caring about his story, or his wife, or why they had no children, or how many other mothers through the years sat in this very chair and listened to terrible, terrible news about their children. They had nothing to do with me or David, and I felt guilty for not caring, but it didn't matter. Guilt is a hollow motivation. It doesn't last; instead it lingers like an odor.

"I think I'd like to go home now, please."

We rode in silence back through the grey day. When we passed the school again, the little boy who had been alone under the tree was gone. I wondered where he was, but I didn't think about it very long. There were other things to think about. It was time for me to go home.

CHRIS 2:1

AFTER BETH ANDERSON DISAPPEARED AND THE door closed, Jesus and I sat looking in the direction where she'd been. Neither of us spoke for at least a count of ten, which is an exceptional period of time to sit silently in a room with another person.

I asked, "You know, why would your God, all-knowing, all-loving, do that to one of his children? Why would he have a perfectly nice seven-year-old boy cracked in the head with a baseball bat, on a perfectly normal spring day, turning him into a brain-damaged lost soul and decimating the lives around him?"

I turned to the man who looked like Jesus and continued, "Why? Because if I had a child, and I was all-knowing, and all-loving, and all-powerful, I couldn't do that to one of my children. And if I couldn't do it, a flawed human as I am, how could your God do it?"

He looked at me thoughtfully, waiting for my anger to subside.

"It's not that simple, Chris."

"Really? I can tell you this much: this would have been a much better story if you'd turned out to be David Anderson."

He asked, "It's a better story for me to be David Anderson than Jesus Christ?"

I felt myself losing patience. "You aren't Jesus Christ!"

He leaned back a bit in his chair. He said, "Explain to me what people expected to happen when I returned. Did they expect a ball of fire in the sky, or some type of announcement from the Heavens in a hundred different languages?

"Explain it to me so that I can understand," he said calmly. "A world full of Christians, the foundation of their belief is my return to Earth, and yet people are afraid to follow their faith."

I said, "Then I guess the question becomes, are they Christians at all? I mean, if they don't recognize you, or have the strength to overcome their fears or doubts, then maybe that's your answer. Maybe there's nobody left here worth saving."

"What about you?" he asked.

"I don't believe there's a God, and so I don't believe you could be the Son of God. No father, no son."

He waited for me to continue. "What do we all have in common?" I asked. "Death, dying, mortality. As soon as we are old enough to grasp the concept, we are slapped in the face with futility. Everybody dies. Everybody ends up dead. Good people die and bad people die, just the same. The honest, hardworking, God-loving, loyal father and husband dies in the end along with the lying, stealing, piece-of-shit father.

"It's brutal. So how, as humans, do we cope with this absolute knowledge? We coped by inventing a higher power. Somebody far greater and far smarter than us must have a plan, right? There must be a life after this life—Heaven, a reward, a purpose behind the futility, right?

"God. Buddha. Lots of different people, lots of different forms. All designed and imagined for the purpose of helping us cope with the dark, ultimate truth about our existence. Death waits. There are no exceptions."

He seemed to think about what I'd said, and quietly responded, "So let me ask you a question, much like the one you asked me earlier about why God would have David Anderson hit in the head with a baseball bat.

"You're a smart man, Chris. Educated, intelligent. If you have the ability to believe in something that gives you comfort, that makes your life less frustrating, why would you not allow yourself the comfort of faith in a higher purpose, a reward of a life after this life in a place like Heaven? It seems you are asking the wrong questions."

I said, "So what you're saying is not why should I believe, but why should I not believe?"

"Expect more, Chris."

He was convincing. If I didn't know better, I might have believed he was who he said he was. I decided to move the conversation in another direction.

"Are you going to plead guilty?"

"Of course."

"Do you have a lawyer yet?"

"Not yet. They say one will be appointed for me if I can't afford a lawyer."

I said, "I've heard that people raising money for you might get you out on bail this afternoon. Maybe they'll find you a lawyer today."

"I hope if I get out we can continue our conversation in a nicer place."

"I'm sure two nights in jail is plenty. But I don't know how much longer I'll be here. There's always another story to cover somewhere."

He smiled. "I think if you'll stay with this story a little longer, you'll be glad you did."

The photograph in the column had caused quite a reaction. The editor hadn't expected it. It was just a matter of how long Stanley wanted me to stay.

"You know they're gonna find out who the other bank robber is sooner or later," I said.

"What would be the purpose of that?"

"Because he broke the law. He robbed a bank. They'll want to put him in prison. In fact, they might give you a better plea deal if you'll give up his name. You won't have to stay in prison as long."

"I don't think that would be fair, do you?"

"What's fair got to do with it? If you don't cut a deal now, before they catch the guy on their own, you'll lose your leverage."

"Leverage?" he asked.

"Just think about it. It would be dumb to spend all of those extras years locked up. They're gonna catch him anyway. It's just a matter of when. I've got some ideas myself."

We were at the end of our allotted time.

I asked, "Is there any particular message you'd like me to share? There will be another article tomorrow. This may be your last chance before the world changes the channel."

He smiled. "I trust you, Chris. You'll find the words, and I look forward to our next conversation."

I found myself feeling the same. "Me, too," I said, but I wasn't completely sure we'd have another conversation.

"I'll see you at the bond hearing this afternoon," I said.

BECKY 1:1

SOME PEOPLE DON'T THINK I'M SMART. "Her face doesn't look right, so she must be dumb," they think. Ugly equals dumb. That's what some people think.

I made a 27 on my ACT a few years ago in high school. I would have gone to college with everybody else except I got married and had a baby, but I've got a good job at the bank, with good benefits, and Saturdays pay time and a half if I work a full week.

My life was pretty normal until that morning Jesus robbed my bank. Things happen for a reason. People end up where they end up because it's all part of the plan, and I ended up in that exact bank at that exact time because that's where I was supposed to be.

Marjorie Comstock was scheduled to work that Saturday morning. She called the night before to see if I could switch days. Her kid had a soccer game or something, I don't remember, but it's not really important. What's important is where I ended up when Jesus came through the door and stood there in front of me.

I knew He wasn't there to hurt anybody. I knew He wasn't there to steal our money. He came back for a much higher purpose than anything like that, and being put in that exact place, at that exact time, meant I was selected to do what I was supposed to do.

The man from the newspaper and Chief Bastrop asked me lots of questions. I won't help them. I won't testify against Jesus, and I don't care whether or not they find the man with the weird boat-captain glasses and the silver wedding ring. Whoever he is, Jesus picked him, and that's good enough for me.

At first, I couldn't figure out what I was chosen to do. I was lying in bed the next morning staring at the water stain on the ceiling, the stain I've told my husband, Roger, to paint a hundred thousand times. That's when I figured out I was supposed to help spread the word Jesus was back by starting a website and getting the money to get him out on bail. It just came to me. Popped into my head.

My cousin's husband is a lawyer. I think he does

stuff like divorce papers, but he's the only lawyer I know. His name is Jay Mason, and he has commercials on TV standing in front of lots of law books. The camera zooms in on his face at the end, and he always says, "Know your rights."

I told Jay I was the one who put the bank video on the Internet. People needed to see. Images are powerful. It was the bank video of Jesus standing at the door that stirred people up. We got contributions from all over the country, even one from Israel, to get together the bond money.

I told my husband, "I'll fix up the basement. He can stay down there except when He needs to come upstairs to use the bathroom."

My husband said, "If he's really Jesus, he won't need to use the bathroom."

My husband is an idiot sometimes. He doesn't like the idea of letting Jesus live in our house. He says it will confuse the kids.

"It'll confuse the kids," he said, "and think how much it will cost to feed the man."

I said, "Shut up."

Whenever I tell him to shut up, he shuts up. Besides, I make more money than him anyway. Roger works at the hardware store. He wears one of those dumb aprons and tells people all day how to fix things, mostly rich people with nothing else to do.

When we were in high school, Roger was the first boy to ever look at me the way boys sometimes look at girls. I guess pretty girls get used to it, but it was new for me and so I did anything he wanted me to do, and during Thanksgiving of our senior year in high school he got me pregnant. I think it happened upstairs in his grandmother's house after pumpkin pie. I could hear the men downstairs screaming at the football game on television.

After everybody found out at school, I remember sitting alone during P.E. behind the bleachers. Two boys were talking above me. One of them said, "I can't believe that girl Becky is pregnant."

The other boy said, "Yeah, how drunk would you have to be to fuck that hound?"

I didn't say anything. I just sat there, and when the bell rang I didn't go back to class, ever. I got married, got my GED, had my baby, and then another one, and found this job at the bank. Every Sunday I sit with my family in the same place at church, up front.

The week before Jesus robbed my bank, the preacher gave a sermon about how we never know what God has in store for us, and so we have to be ready when the call comes.

The preacher was right, and when my call came, I was ready. Super ready.

BECKY 1:2

J AY PICKED ME UP IN FRONT of my house so that we could go to the bond hearing together. I'd never been in court before except for the time I called the police on Roger because he threw a fork at me. I can't even remember now what we were fighting about. We had to go to court and ask for the charges to be dropped. The judge didn't seem too happy about it.

Jay's car was fancy and blue. It smelled like cigarette smoke, which I think is disgusting, but it's his car so I guess he can do what he wants in it.

Jay said, "Look, I don't do much criminal work, but this is a good opportunity, obviously, for some free publicity. Eddie called to say there's tons of cameras and reporters staked out outside the courthouse.

"I need you to let me do the talking, Becky. Don't

give any interviews now. Don't tell anybody we're related.

"If I can get the guy out of jail, we'll do a little media blitz thing, get on a few talk shows, whatever."

He looked different than he does in the commercials. Whiter. More nervous. He rolled down his window a few inches and lit a Marlboro cigarette.

I asked, "Will I need to do anything in court?"

"I don't know. Maybe. You might have to tell the judge where you live, where the defendant will stay, stuff like that."

He took a puff of his cigarette and added, "I know you think he's Jesus and everything, but for right now keep that to yourself. Just be a good citizen, willing to help a guy down on his luck by giving him a place to stay and a few meals."

I watched his mouth move. It moved kinda funny, like the words were coming out faster than he was speaking. Kinda the way it does on television when the sound and the picture are off a little bit.

"Okay?" he asked.

"Okay," I answered.

We parked in front of the courthouse. Like Jay said, there where TV trucks and cameras set up around the steps leading to the front door. We walked right past them and nobody asked any questions, because I guess they didn't know who we were.

Jay said to me, "I'll give my press conference on the way out."

He brushed his hand across the shoulder of his suit and straightened his tie at the neck. It was the same tie he wore in his commercials, or at least it was one just like it. He pushed his hand in his pants pocket. He pulled out two pills and shoved them in his mouth, leaning down to drink from the water fountain. The pills were white.

The courtroom was scary and quiet. There were lots of people sitting inside, but Jesus and the judge weren't there yet.

Jay asked me to sit in the front row behind the table where he would be with Jesus. I saw Chief Bastrop, and the man from the newspaper, and my manager from the bank, Mr. Tinsley. I hadn't thought about him being mad at me for giving Jesus a place to stay, but it didn't matter if he was mad or not. This was bigger than the bank. This was bigger than me or my job or Mr. Tinsley.

When they brought Jesus in the courtroom He had handcuffs and chains on His feet. He reminded me of those pictures of Jesus carrying the cross on His shoulders with the Roman guards pushing and prodding Him with sticks and spears. I wanted to yell out. But then He looked at me and I felt all my anger flow from my body like water. It was that same peaceful feeling I had in the bank that day, except with one difference. I felt a warmth inside me, all over me, a tingle in certain places.

They put Him in the chair next to Jay, and I could hear them whispering, but I couldn't hear what it was about. There were noises around me, people shuffling papers, low talking, and when the judge came into the room a man said, "All rise."

The judge was a black man. He looked like a grand-father, maybe seventy years old, with grey hair and soft eyes. Something about the way he moved reminded me of a St. Bernard. Clumsy, but soft-hearted and gentle. Kinda bushy.

He said, "Be seated. We've got a bond hearing this afternoon. John Doe. Robbery in the first degree. Been in jail two days. What says the State?"

A man with a pointy face and a dark suit stood at the other table.

"Your Honor, we'd ask the Court to deny bail, or in the alternative to set bond at one million dollars. Even with diligent efforts, we've been unable to determine the identity of the defendant. There are no fingerprints in the criminal system. There's no DNA match in the database. He has no identification and claims he's Jesus."

The judge looked at Jesus.

"I can see the resemblance," the judge said. There was a low murmur behind me.

The man in the dark suit continued, "This was a robbery with a weapon. We believe there was an accomplice, but there's been no arrest, and the defendant has not yet cooperated in that regard.

"He has no residence in the county, no family, no job, no roots to keep him here, and we believe he's a flight risk."

The judge turned to look at Jay.

"Mr. Mason, are you the defendant's attorney?"

Jay said, his voice low, "Yes sir, at the present time."

"What says the defense?" the judge asked.

Jesus said, "I'd like to plead guilty, please."

"No, no," Jay said, and turned to his client. "We talked about that. Not now. This is just a bond hearing."

The judge stepped in. He spoke calmly and directly to Jesus. "There will be plenty of time for that. You'll have an arraignment date set, and we'll take a plea then. I just want to hear arguments about whether you need to stay in jail or get out until the next hearing."

The judge said again to Jay, "What says the defense?"

"Well, Your Honor, a member of our community, in good standing, Mrs. Becky Sullivan, has agreed to provide my client a place to stay in her home.

"Obviously, the man doesn't have a history of being a criminal or his fingerprints would be in the system. Obviously, there would be a match in the DNA database. He can't alter his fingerprints or DNA.

"The gun Mr. Thomas alluded to was an unloaded pellet gun. If he caused such terrible fear, I don't think one of the bank tellers, Mrs. Sullivan, would let him in her home with her family.

"I believe if the defendant is equipped with an ankle bracelet the Court can ensure he'll be here for these proceedings without keeping the man locked up in jail at taxpayers' expense."

The look on the faces of the men at the other table made me think Jay was doing a better job than they expected.

The judge got quiet. He looked around the room. His eyes stopped on me.

"Are you Mrs. Sullivan?"

I stood. "Yes, sir." I could feel all the eyes in the room on me.

"Is that right? Are you willing to let this man live in your home during the duration of this case? It could be months and months."

"Yes, sir," I said. "I fixed up the basement. He can stay down there and come upstairs to use the bathroom. We've got cable."

Jay interrupted, "Your Honor, without revealing our defense, if the Court is inclined to set a reasonable bond, we would agree to a mental evaluation."

I looked at Jesus. He smiled, and then looked down at His hands cuffed together in His lap. How nice it must be to never worry, I thought, to always know everything will turn out alright. How comforting.

The courtroom was quiet while we waited. Only Jesus seemed not to care what the judge would say. It didn't concern Him, almost like we were all there for somebody else. Like He just happened to be sitting at the table with leg chains and handcuffs.

The judge said, "Well, I think we'll give it a try. Bond is set at $25,000, property or corporate surety are acceptable. The defendant will be confined to the residence of Mrs. Sullivan, he'll be required to wear an ankle monitor twenty-four hours a day, and also undergo a mental health evaluation."

I felt Mr. Tinsley staring at me from across the room. I stared right back at him until he turned away first. I would not be intimidated. For some reason it made me think about that boy in high school above me in the bleachers that day. Where was he now, I thought to myself. Where was he on this very important day when Jesus was coming to live in my basement?

BECKY 1:3

AFTER THE CRAZINESS OUTSIDE THE COURTHOUSE, inside Jay's car it was suddenly very quiet. It didn't seem real I could be sitting in the back seat next to Jesus.

Like an idiot, the first thing I said was, "Do you like lasagna?"

"Yes," He answered, and smiled.

"I'll make lasagna for supper. It's probably been a long time since you've had a home-cooked meal. Roger hates lasagna, but so what. He can have leftovers if he doesn't like it. I like lasagna, the kind with lots of white cheese."

There was already a TV truck parked in front of my house with a big camera on a tripod outside near the sidewalk. Roger and the kids were standing on the front porch when we pulled into the driveway.

Jay said to Jesus, "I'll handle the interviews. We'll get you an exclusive on a big-time news show. I've already gotten a few offers. We'll talk about it tomorrow after you get yourself a little rest."

Jesus said, "Am I allowed to play golf?"

Jay looked at him awful funny-like. "No. You're on house arrest. You can't leave the house or that thing on your ankle will alert the sheriff's office."

I jumped in, "Don't worry. There's plenty to do. Roger's got one of those golf video games, and there's a basketball goal in the backyard. Do you like basketball?"

"Not really," He said.

Down in the basement, I couldn't tell whether Jesus was disappointed. He just laid down on the bed and asked if He could be alone for a while.

"Will they bring your things later?"

"I don't have any things," He said.

"No toothbrush? No clothes?"

He didn't answer.

"I'll go upstairs and start the lasagna. Are you okay?" I asked.

"Yes, and thank you for having me in your home, Becky."

I smiled. "You're welcome," I said, and felt that feeling again. The warmth, like being under a big brown blanket. A sense of relief, like everything has already been decided, and the worry left me like a breath. I closed my eyes and turned to leave.

At the top of the stairs, Roger said, "What's for dinner?"

"Lasagna."

"I hate lasagna."

"I know. Jesus loves it."

"What do I get?"

"Whatever you can find."

"How long is he going to be living in our basement?"

I turned on him. "As long as He wants to," I yelled. "It's Jesus, you idiot, and all you can think about is what's for dinner."

Roger suddenly looked disgusting. He was uglier and fatter than I had ever noticed before. His teeth were crooked. His hair was receding. I couldn't believe we were married, or he was the father of my children, or I'd ever let him climb on top of me.

"It doesn't seem fair," he said pitifully.

LATER THAT NIGHT, AFTER JESUS ATE lasagna in His room, He asked to see the newspaper. He wanted to read the article written by the man from the *New York Times*.

We sat side by side on the bed. When I handed him the newspaper, I said, "I'm sorry I cut out your picture. It's a really good picture. I taped it on my bathroom mirror so it's one of the first things I see in the morning."

"What are they saying about me on television?" He asked.

"Mostly they argue about whether or not you're really Jesus. One person yells about how he knows for sure that you're really Jesus, and another person yells back about how it can't be proven and they should do a DNA test or something."

He didn't say anything. I continued, "The enemy tries to steal the mystery of miracles with scientific explanations. I think the Devil loves a good explanation."

Jesus said, "There are those who would agree with you. For in much wisdom is much grief: and he that increaseth knowledge increaseth sorrow."

I wanted to move closer to Him. I scooted over a few inches. Through the fabric of clothing, our legs touched. I was afraid, but then not afraid at the same time. It wasn't my decision.

We sat quietly while He read the newspaper article to himself. Finally Jesus said, "What proof do they need?"

"You're sitting right here. Right in front of me. That's all the evidence any Christian should need. If they don't believe in you then they'll go to hell forever."

"Does Roger believe?" He asked.

I hesitated. "No."

"Do you think he should go to hell for eternity?"

I answered, "That's what the Bible says."

Jesus explained, "I didn't write the Bible. Men wrote the Bible."

We sat next to each other for what seemed like a minute, our legs still touching. I'd never felt in my whole life the way He made me feel. Never, not for a single minute.

"Would you like some more lasagna?" I asked. "There's plenty."

We were alone, and neither of us moved. I felt lightheaded, and I'm embarrassed to say it, but I felt a warmth down there, a wetness, a need.

NEIL 2:1

I T'S THE NEVER-ENDING BALANCE. ON ONE side is the absolute knowledge that nothing whatsoever matters. There's nothing any of us can do, nothing, that makes any difference at all. The world will continue to spin, time will continue to run, and each of us, every single one of us, will die, go back into the earth one way or another, and be forgotten in the blink of an eye.

On the other side, we wake up every morning and convince ourselves how important it is to provide for our children, bring the dog inside when it's cold, mow the grass, pay the electric bill. And we ignore the irreconcilable differences between the two, the dichotomy. How can we not? Utter hopelessness is only a thought away, and the dogs are at the door.

The night of the robbery I sat in the living room

just trying to breathe normally. The local news channel showed the bank.

"What kind of a loser robs a bank dressed like Jesus?" my wife said.

The police chief, with a microphone held in front of his face by the thin hand of an attractive female reporter, said, "We believe there's an accomplice."

My wife added, "And what kind of a loser robs a bank with a loser dressed like Jesus?"

My daughter, Gina, giggled dismissively. "Especially when the grand total of your heist is $2,781." She looked at me. "It smells bad in here," Gina said to no one in particular.

I couldn't smell anything. I'd lied earlier and told my wife I wasn't feeling well to avoid eating dinner. "What's done is done," I kept repeating to myself, but I felt like throwing up. I guess it wasn't a lie.

The checklist ran over and over in my mind. I'd thrown the clothes and sunglasses in a Dumpster across town. The pellet pistol was at the bottom of a small man-made lake two miles in the other direction. The cash, apparently $2,781, was in a bag shoved in the corner of my toolshed behind the power washer I'd never used.

My wife and daughter left me alone in the room.

Chief Bastrop said, "We believe it's a local job. It's just a matter of time until we identify both robbers. One is in custody and might cooperate. It's just a matter of time."

My other daughter, Elise, came down the stairs. At seventeen she looks so much like my wife people call them sisters. When she was little, we were best friends. I think sometimes my wife, Amanda, was jealous we spent so much time together, laughing, driving around, going to movies. But then she got older and started looking more like Amanda, and one day when she was about thirteen, Elise turned and looked at me with the same hate I'd seen in her mother's eyes for all those years. I knew our time together was over. She would resent me, and I would resent her back, and except for old photographs, we'd both forget what it was like before.

Elise said, "I'm going out."

"Where are you going?" I asked.

She tilted her head like her mother. Her mouth drew up tight like it always does before she says something angry.

"If you have to know, I'll tell you. I'm going to the country club with Elizabeth. She's a member. I'm not. It's embarrassing. Every time we go she has to sign me in as a guest, get a guest pass. They look at me different. And I always say, 'I think we'll be joining soon.' Which is a big, fat lie."

I watched her mouth move. I thought of the money in the toolshed. Just enough to pay the $2,500 membership deposit. Just enough to buy a few weeks worth of smiles until she realized Elizabeth has a nicer car, a bigger playroom, a better life.

Chief Bastrop said, "Take a look at this picture from the bank security camera of the man we believe to be the accomplice, and if you recognize him call the Police Department."

Elise looked at the television. The picture of me was blurry. The sunglasses and hat hid part of my face, but you could see the curve of my cheekbone.

Elise looked back at me, and then back at the television. There was a moment I thought she would say it. I thought she would say, "You're the bank robber. You robbed the bank."

Instead, her cell phone made a noise. She lifted it in front of her face, apparently forgot about our conversation or the bank robbery, and walked out the front door.

Why did I write "Nick Blankenship" on the deposit slip? Why did I leave the pillow in the woods? Would it have my DNA on it? And would Jesus talk? Would he tell on me? That was the biggest problem. I'd go to prison. Why did he need me in the first place? Was it the plan all along to have someone for him to point the finger at? A bargaining chip? A way to spread his message and avoid going to jail while I took the fall?

I left the living room, walked in the darkness to the toolshed, and felt the bag of money in the corner. I shoved it under my shirt and made it to the car parked in the driveway.

I sat in my car and felt the vomit churn in my stomach. The money had to be buried somewhere with no connection to me. It had to be far away. I reached down and felt the cool metal of the pistol under my car seat. It held hope like it always did, and as I sat in the driveway alone, the gun in my lap, my stomach began to settle.

CHRIS 3:1

ECKY TOLD ME SHE RECOGNIZED THE shirt of the second robber. She believed it was a shirt she donated to Goodwill. I drove to the location on Jacoby Street where Becky said she made the donation, and sat in the parking lot gathering my thoughts before I entered the store.

My phone rang. It was my editor, Stanley.

"So, the lady from California ended up a dead end?" he said.

"Yeah, she said it wasn't her son. It would've been a good story if it was."

"I've got something else for you. This is a bit different. It's off the record, and I mean totally off the record. You understand?"

Stanley had never said anything like that to me.

"Okay," I said.

"I got a call from a guy I've known a long time. He's been a source for me for many years, but also a friend of mine. He's with the White House now."

"The White House?" I repeated.

"Yeah, his name is Ted Foster. He called me, wants to meet with you this afternoon. Same place, your hotel, except not in the lobby. Two o'clock. I'll call you and let you know what room it is."

"I don't understand," I said. "What does the White House have to do with anything?"

"Your story on this Jesus Bandit has gotten a lot of attention, Chris. I want you to meet with Ted, but your meeting, and whatever's said in that meeting, won't be part of your story down there. You hear me?"

I hesitated. "I hear you. I don't understand, but I hear you."

He said, "I'll call you back with the room number." Then he hung up.

A GIRL, MAYBE TWENTY, STOOD BEHIND the counter at the Goodwill store. There were just a few customers milling around the place.

She was overweight, plain, without a wedding ring, and her hair was pulled back on one side, held with a barrette. Her clothes looked like they'd come from the racks in the store, and she had the appearance of a girl who could rest her head on the counter and fall asleep in only a few seconds.

"Hi," I said.

She looked at me, and responded the same. "Hi."

"I'm Chris," I said, and held out my hand.

She looked down at my outstretched hand, and reluctantly said, "I'm Tiffany."

Her handshake was limp and warm, like holding a fold of elephant skin. She looked like she'd rather be almost anywhere else on Earth, but no matter where she found herself, she'd wish she was somewhere else.

"I'm from the *New York Times*. I'm doing a story on that guy who robbed the bank. The guy who thinks he's Jesus. Have you heard about it?"

"I saw something on TV," she said.

"I need your help," I said. "This is important. Your help could be important to the story, figuring out who this guy really is."

She just stood there.

I said, "You'd really be helping with the investigation."

Finally, after what seemed like a millennium, she asked, "What kind of help?"

"Okay, we think the second robber, the guy who worked with the guy who thinks he's Jesus, was in your store a few days before the robbery. We think he might have bought a shirt."

"What's he look like?" she asked.

"Well, that's the problem. We don't know. He was kind of wearing a disguise. We're hoping to get a look at his face from your security cameras. I see you've got cameras around the store."

She cast her eyes around like she'd never noticed before, stopping on one camera and then moving to the next.

"I don't know nothing about the cameras. I've seen my manager watching the monitors sometimes and doing the computer. You'll have to ask her."

"Is she here?"

"She don't come in until lunch today."

"Well, I'm sure she wouldn't have a problem with it. I could just burn a copy of those two or three days. It won't take me long. I've done this before."

She just stood there again. I felt the girl might lapse into a coma.

"I don't know about that. I could get in trouble."

"No," I said. "You won't get in trouble. I'll be out of here way before lunch."

I pulled my wallet from my back pocket, removed a one hundred dollar bill, and placed it on the counter between us underneath my hand, where she could see it was a hundred dollar bill, but the cameras couldn't.

She needed it. She needed it badly. I waited.

Tiffany looked around the store. She glanced up at one of the cameras.

I whispered, "You won't get in trouble. Just pretend you're giving me change for a dollar. Put the bill in your pocket, open the register, and pretend to give me four quarters. The register will be right at the end of the day."

Her fat hand covered mine, and the bill was exchanged. I followed Tiffany to the back room.

"Eddie and Mr. Carl are in the back unloading. Just hurry up and leave here."

Ten minutes later I was in my car with what I needed, headed back to my hotel to see what I could see and then meet with the mystery man from the White House.

CHRIS 3:2

ACK IN MY ROOM I STARTED the process of watching the Goodwill security disc. There would be hours and hours of watching, hoping to see a man, white, late thirties to early forties, roaming around the store and then picking out a shirt. Not just any shirt, but the shirt Becky Sullivan recognized. The shirt the other robber wore in the bank that day, hopefully leading to the man who might hold the key to identifying Jesus and wrapping up the story in a nice, neat ball.

Stanley called. "Ted will meet you in room 132. Don't bring your tape recorder."

"Okay," I said, but before I could finish he hung up on the other end.

I walked through the lobby, looking at the signs on

the wall for directions to room 132. I noticed a man on the couch watching me. In fact, as I pretended not to notice him, I saw several people who seemed to be just hanging around. A young woman in a chair waiting for no one. A large black man by the door with a phone to his ear.

The first man I noticed left the couch and followed me down the hall to room 132. I turned to face him, and he made a gesture to lift my arms parallel to the floor. I did as he requested, and the man patted me down quickly and efficiently.

He knocked twice on the door. A voice from inside said, "Come in."

The man stayed outside in the hallway. I closed the door behind me to face another man.

"I'm Ted Foster," he said, before I had to wonder. "Stanley tells me good things about you."

He was about sixty, maybe sixty-five, thin, grey hair, shorter than me. There was something about his clothes. Like he was trying to be casual, but he wasn't a casual man. He was a serious man, and my curiosity overflowed.

"Lots of mystery," I said. "Guys patting me down."

Ted Foster took a sip of coffee from his dark blue mug. He moved slowly, almost elegantly. He didn't waste time.

"You know, when I first met Stanley, thirty years ago, the news business was different. There was a bond between the news-maker and the news reporter that doesn't exist much anymore. When Stanley tells me you're a man I can talk to off the record, I believe him. Old school, I think they say these days."

"Old school," I repeated, for no real reason.

We stood and looked at each other.

Finally, he said, "I need you to say it."

"Say what?" I asked.

"I need you to say our conversation is off the record. Man to man."

I didn't have a choice, of course. If I didn't say it, the guy from the hallway would be escorting me away. So I said it: "Our conversation is off the record."

"Thank you," he said, and smiled the sort of smile I hadn't seen in a long time. The smile of a man who gets what he wants one way or another, and if you don't understand it from the beginning the price you'll pay can be more than you can afford.

"Chris, this guy, the Jesus Bandit, tell me about him."

"There's not a whole lot to tell other than what I wrote in the paper."

His eyes were cold, bright blue. Almost too blue

for a man his age. He didn't get where he was without a remarkable amount of patience, and so he just waited for me to say more.

"He's maybe early thirties," I said. "He looks like you'd expect Jesus to look. No tattoos, no fingerprints in the system, no DNA in the database, no forms of identification, no home, and nobody to this point who's been able to come forward and tell us anything about him."

Mr. Foster said, "It seems to me he didn't expect to get away with the robbery."

"It seems that way. He just stood there until the police arrived. No disguise, no getaway car found, an unloaded pellet gun."

"Then why'd he do it?" he asked.

"He says he did it to get the world's attention. Kind of a modern-day announcement that Jesus has returned to save your soul, so get ready."

Ted Foster sat down in a chair and motioned for me to sit across the coffee table from him. He looked even smaller in the chair than he'd looked standing up, almost effeminate.

"You believe in God, Chris?" he asked.

"No, sir. I don't."

He said, "Our president does. He believes in God

with every molecule of his mind and body."

I said, "I think we're all aware what Henry Davidson believes. When you run on a platform of faith, and you use the phrase 'Bible-based' in speeches over three hundred times in the campaign, I think you've pretty much let the cat out of the bag about your religious leanings."

He took another slow sip of his coffee and then set the blue mug down, soundless, on the glass tabletop.

"The president was captivated by the photograph you took."

I couldn't quite figure out the purpose of the conversation.

"Where is this going?" I asked impatiently.

Mr. Foster slowly turned his head to the window, and said, "He'd like to meet the man, and we'd like you to arrange it."

I said the first thing that entered my crowded mind. "Is this a joke?"

"No, Mr. Young, it's not a joke. The president's faith is not a joke. Who are you to decide? Since you've met him, and established rapport with him, and we can count on your silence, you're the perfect man for the job."

"Are you serious?" I asked. "Are we seriously debating whether this man is the Son of God, Jesus Christ? Because just yesterday we were debating whether he's a brain-damaged little boy grown up and lost. And now the president of the United States wants to meet the man, and I can't even write about it."

He turned and looked at me. "That pretty much sums it up."

I said, "If he's so sure of his faith, why does this have to be a big secret?"

Ted Foster's voice changed. His eyes narrowed. "We've got no interest, Mr. Young, in being mocked by the media. The president wants to meet the man to learn more, not because he's ready to run off to the Promised Land quite yet."

The blue in his eyes had become darker. I wondered, in the last thirty years, how many stories in the *New York Times* had come from this man and what his motivation had been for each. I'm not easily intimidated, but Ted Foster left me intimidated.

I said, "I'll have to call Chief Bastrop and set up a meeting. He'll have to call the lawyer."

"Leave the lawyer out of it. The fewer people, the better. I understand he's staying at a woman's house, Becky Sullivan. We'd like to meet at her house, late tonight, preferably in a room with no windows. We've already secured an avenue to arrive at the house through the backyard to avoid the cameras on the street."

I asked, "Who's allowed at this meeting?"

"You, me, the president, Becky Sullivan, and if we have to, Chief Bastrop."

It was all strange and unbelievable. The president was somewhere in the area, which explained the Secret Service in the lobby. In just a few hours I'd be sitting in a room with him, a room in Becky Sullivan's house, watching the president of my country having a conversation with a man I believed to be a mentally ill, Jesus look-alike bank robber with a hygiene problem. And I'd given my word it was off the record.

"Is this for real?" I asked Ted Foster.

He smiled that smile again.

"Yes, Mr. Young, this is for real."

HENRY 1:1

I WAS BORN IN A SMALL town in the middle of America. I know it sounds hard to believe, but on my fifth birthday my grandfather asked me what I wanted to be when I grew up.

"I'll be the president of the United States," I said.

My grandfather asked, "Is that what you want to be?"

"No," I answered, "but that's what I'll be anyway."

I CAN'T IMAGINE WHAT LIFE WOULD be like without the faith that God has a plan for me, all mapped out from beginning to end, and all I have to do each morning is get out of bed and believe. There's nothing to debate. It's not a mystery novel where clues are laid side by side until we arrive at the truth. Once you've seen the truth, it can't be unseen, and we need no proof of the existence of something we know exists.

All my adult life I've started each day with a cup of coffee, a few minutes of Bible verses, and the morning newspaper. This ritual didn't change when I was elected president. Of course, I would wake up in different places around the world, but at least the first thirty minutes of each day was always the same.

I remember the morning I was looking through the *New York Times* and saw the face of the man who proclaimed He was Jesus Christ. There was something about His photograph that made me look closer and then led me to read the article. I set the paper off to the side when I was finished, but later I was drawn back and actually cut it out carefully.

I've always been able to rely on Ted Foster. I may be a religious man, but I'm not naïve. They are very different sides of the same coin. Ted is a political insider. He gets things done that need to get done. He sees the world in a useful way. It's not my way, but it's useful for a man in my position.

I handed him the folded newspaper article. After he was finished reading he looked at me the way a mother might look at a child she knows is tempted to do something of which she doesn't approve.

Ted waited for me to speak.

"I want to meet Him," I said.

"I know you do," Ted answered, "but it's not a good idea."

"Well, Ted, if Jesus decided it was a good idea to come back and save our souls, yours included, then how could it not be a good idea for the leader of the free world to go see the man?"

Ted looked back down at the article in his hands. "Mr. President, he's just another whack-job. Some poor bastard who thinks he's Jesus this week and Batman next week. If you go down to meet this guy and it ends up with the press, you'll look as crazy as him, maybe crazier."

I sat down behind my desk, and Ted sat down across from me. I knew his mind was spinning with ideas of how to get me down there to see the man in jail without the press finding out.

I said, "Well, Ted, how do you think Jesus will come back?"

He looked resigned. "We've had conversations like this one before. They don't go well."

"Tell me," I said, "do you think there will be a big explosion in the sky and Jesus will parachute down like those guys who land on the football field at halftime?"

I continued, "Or maybe we'll hear music. Everybody will hear the same heavenly music."

"Maybe," Ted said.

"I don't think so, Ted. I think it'll be just like this. He'll come back like a man on the street, and we'll be tested to believe. Just like this man in jail, He'll have no matching fingerprints, or relatives stepping forward. He'll be forced, in our mixed-up society, to do something outlandish like robbing a bank to get anybody's attention. That's how I think Jesus will come back."

Ted looked into my eyes. "Mr. President, a living dog is better than a dead lion."

I smiled. "I always like when you quote scripture, Mr. Foster. And I agree with that."

"I don't," he said. "The most important asset the president holds is his credibility. If you go chasing saviors in county jails, you'll lose that credibility with the people. It's not about re-election. It's about people feeling secure. People knowing their leader is dependable."

I tilted my neck to the side, stretching the muscles around the place I'd had surgery six months earlier. It was sore, and ached most days depending on how I'd slept the night before. Sometimes, if I tilted it just right, there was a small popping sound that gave relief.

"I agree with you," I said. "But I'm going anyway.

There's something leading me there and I can't ignore it because somebody else might make fun of me.

"Do whatever you need to do, Ted, to get me in and out of there without eroding the trust of the American people. I need to talk to the man face to face."

Ted looked at me. I could almost hear the wheels in his head turning with the details of flights, hotels, and contacts. There was not much that Ted Foster couldn't get done. He was a modern-day hit man, without the bodies.

I said, "You know what you remind me of, Ted? A modern-day hit man, without the bodies."

His face was expressionless as he rose from his chair and handed me the article. I watched him walk from the room, leaving me alone.

It was the light. The light in the photograph did something to his face. It looked like a painting of Jesus I'd seen when I was a little boy. It was the first impression of the image of my Lord and Savior, Jesus Christ, the Son of God, and if this man in jail was just another whack-job like Ted Foster said, then so be it, but I would not ignore the calling. It wasn't my choice.

HENRY 1:2

FOR SECURITY REASONS, CHRIS YOUNG, TED Foster, and Chief Bastrop went ahead of me to the house where the meeting would take place, in the home of Becky Sullivan. While I waited I scanned the television channels and settled on a local news show.

Chief Bastrop, in a taped interview, sat behind his desk. He seemed to be a man whose patience was tested with each question.

"Have you been able to utilize videotapes from the cameras around the Wal-Mart and the grocery store parking lots to identify the second robber?" the lady reporter asked.

"One of the tapes was apparently erased accidently. The other is of very poor quality. I expect the man we have in custody already to help us in identifying the second robber and making an arrest in the near future."

"Is the Jesus Bandit cooperating?" she asked.

Chief Bastrop drew a deep breath before answering. "I'd rather not talk about certain aspects of the investigation. It's just a matter of time. And the man out there, the man who still has the money, better be looking over his shoulder."

I WAS DRIVEN TO A VACANT house behind the house of Becky Sullivan. As always, I was briefed about the plans. We would walk to the back entrance of the Sullivan house and the meeting would take place in the basement. The Sullivans were not aware of my arrival, and when we entered the back door, Ted Foster politely introduced me to a man standing in the kitchen.

"Mr. President, this is Roger Sullivan."

The man looked at me and said, mostly to himself, "Holy shit."

"It's nice to meet you, Mr. Sullivan," I replied.

One of the Secret Service agents stayed at the back door. Another remained in the kitchen with Roger Sullivan. I'd long ago stopped worrying about my protection. Everything was always planned down to the last detail, and whatever happened would be God's will anyway. Going to the Sullivan house was a much better idea than trying to meet in the sterile environment of a hotel room or government office.

The basement was not particularly large. Jesus was sitting on the edge of a bed next to a woman. I recognized Chief Bastrop from his TV interview. There were several folding chairs in a semi-circle. Everyone stood when I came down the long flight of wooden stairs.

"Oh my God," the woman said.

I extended my hand to her first. "Thank you for allowing us to visit your home, Mrs. Sullivan."

She managed to say, "You're welcome."

I shook Chief Bastrop's hand, and then the hand of Chris Young from the *Times*, and last I turned to the man I'd come to see.

"How are you?" I asked.

"I'm fine," He said.

Unlike the others, Jesus showed no reaction to my presence. I could just as well have been a neighbor or a friend of the family.

We all sat down. I didn't come for small talk.

I said, "I'm told you wanted to get arrested. Why? Why would anybody want to go to jail, face a possible prison sentence?"

He was very calm. I noticed the bracelet on his ankle with a little red light flashing like a heartbeat.

He said, "Would you be here if I hadn't been arrested? Would you have come all this way to see me if I hadn't been in the newspaper?"

I felt myself drawn to His face.

"No," I said. "I guess I wouldn't have."

We all sat quietly for a moment.

I turned to Ted Foster and said, "Leave us, please."

He started to say, "Mr. President, I'm not sure…"

"Leave us," I repeated. "Just for a few minutes. I need to have a private conversation."

I looked at each of the other people in the room, and one by one they rose and started up the stairs. A long glance at the two Secret Service agents in the room finally ended with the two men leaving me alone with Jesus.

When the door closed above, I said, "Why now? Why come back now?"

He said, "Don't you think it's time? Look around you. Look at the world. There are those who might say I've come too late."

"I'm a Christian," I said.

"I know."

"I believe that God sent His only son to sacrifice His life for our sins, my sins."

He didn't say anything. The basement was extremely quiet, and then I heard a creaking up above, someone walking on the kitchen floor, and as we sat there in silence a feeling arose in me that is difficult to describe.

We just looked at each other. It was close to the sensation we have right before falling asleep. The quiet serenity, without worry, almost like floating above the moment. I felt myself begin to cry softly, free from embarrassment, and I didn't try to hide it.

I will never forget those few simple minutes. I was restored, and I heard myself say, "I believe you're Jesus Christ."

"I know," He said. "Your belief has no more effect on my existence than your friend's disbelief. I am exactly who I am, and that's all."

"My friend?" I asked.

"Mr. Foster. We had a conversation before you arrived."

"How do I convince him?" I asked. "It's no coincidence I'm in the position I'm in at this time in history. I have the opportunity to bring to light your return like no other person alive. How do I convince them? How do I make them know for sure?"

He smiled slightly, the smile of a man who knows more.

He said, "Faith is the substance of things hoped for, the evidence of things not seen. By its definition, there is no proof. You either believe, or you don't. There's no in-between."

"Is that the test?" I asked. "Is that the test of who will be saved? Those who believe blindly and those who question?"

"I don't think of it as a test, Henry. A test is something you pass or fail. Faith is more like a characteristic."

For some reason I blurted out, "How will the world end?"

Jesus hesitated, "I don't know. I'm concerned with the parts, not the whole. My Father will end it as He chooses, just as it all began."

We sat quietly again for several minutes.

I said, "I'm going to have a press conference. I'll announce to the world your return. The president of the United States will announce the return of Jesus, as we all knew would happen.

"People will listen. People will come to you as I have."

He smiled again, and said, "To put the world in order, we must first put the nation in order; to put the nation in order, we must put the family in order; to put the family in order, we must cultivate our personal life; and to cultivate our personal life, we must first set our hearts right."

When I stood from the chair, I stood too quickly and felt a lightness in my head. Jesus stood, and we hugged. There was a musty smell, and the smell seemed to add to my weakness as I tried to ascend the stairs.

I remember walking up a number of steps. I remember turning and feeling the need to reach for the railing. And then I remember the beginning of my fall.

The next thing I remember was looking up into the face of Jesus. If I had any doubts before then, they were all gone away with His face. There was a light around Him, a low yellow light, just like the photograph, and then I woke up in the hospital with Ted Foster by my bed.

HENRY 1:3

"WHAT HAPPENED?" I ASKED TED FOSTER. My head hurt. The hospital room was small and dimly lit. I could vaguely feel the presence of other people passing in and out.

"You fell," he said. "You passed out on the stairs and fell down a few steps. Hit your head."

Ted looked very dire, even more serious than usual. He reminded me of my father who long ago sat next to me in a hospital bed when I was just a boy. I'd fallen off the roof of my grandfather's barn and cracked my skull against a fence post. I could see in my father's eyes the fear he felt for me.

Ted said, "They'll run a few tests, then we'll get you to Washington to check everything out."

I said, "It's Him, you know?"

Ted continued without pause, "The doctors will make sure it isn't something serious."

"It's Jesus, Ted. He's come back just like my father said He would. When we get to Washington, you'll schedule a news conference. It's my purpose on this Earth, to tell people, and there's no reason to wait. It's our season of grace, Ted. Do not let it pass." Ted Foster looked at me like I was a child, a child who'd fallen from his grandfather's barn roof and cracked his skull on the fence post, a child unable to separate dreams and demons. But if I was to rise to my destiny and be the teller of news most people would be unable to comprehend, it was a look I'd need to accept as part of my challenge.

"First," he said, "the doctors will do what they need to do, and then we'll talk about it. First, we'll make sure our president is well."

I must have fallen back to sleep, because I was immediately in an airplane, high above, looking down below on the checkered-square landscape of the American heartland. One square, miles wide, was completely engulfed in orange flames.

In the dream I asked Ted Foster, "What's going on down there? Why's the one square in the middle on fire?"

There was no answer.

EDWIN 2:1

A S A POLICE OFFICER, AND LATER the chief of police, I'd seen lots of crazy shit, but I'd never seen anything like the night the president of the United States of America came down the stairs into the basement of Becky Sullivan.

I remember thinking, the president of the United States doesn't come down the stairs into a basement to meet a bank robber who thinks he's Jesus Christ. But come down those stairs he did, wearing blue jeans and a tan sweater, and sat with us like it was a perfectly normal thing to do.

And after he asked us to leave, while I stood upstairs drinking coffee in the kitchen, I remember thinking how could the Secret Service leave them alone down there? Jesus could snap the president's neck in a cold second and leave his body limp on the floor like a rag doll. Then what?

When the noise came from downstairs, the noise a human body makes when it falls freely to the ground, people scrambled in every direction. It was a damn madhouse. I imagined the president dead in the basement below me, but he wasn't dead. They said he'd fallen, hit his head. Ted Foster remained calm, barking out orders that other people followed.

There was a doctor in the group. I guess the president doesn't go anywhere without a doctor. The ambulance arrived without a siren or flashing lights. The remaining members of the press outside the house were wide-eyed. Something was going on. Something newsworthy.

I was told to tell the reporters a family member of the Sullivans had a medical problem. It was a personal matter and nothing to be concerned about. The family wanted their privacy respected.

The ambulance backed all the way around to the rear entrance of the house. One of the reporters asked me, "How'd you get here? Your car's not here, and we didn't see you go inside."

I've never been too good at lying. It's usually more trouble than it's worth, but on this occasion the truth wasn't much of an option.

After the ambulance left I went back inside. Chris Young was in the kitchen, sitting around the small kitchen table with Becky Sullivan and her husband. Becky's eyes were red, and she couldn't stop herself from crying.

Roger Sullivan looked to me for answers. "Why was the president here? Why was the president in our house?"

"I don't completely know, Roger."

He said, "The Secret Service man told us we can't tell anyone. No one. He said if there's a leak, they'll know where it came from because you and this other guy here swore not to tell anyone."

Roger gestured at Chris Young like he was a stranger who'd wandered into his home and sat down at the kitchen table.

I said, "I think you should do what the Secret Service man told you to do. Besides, who'd believe this crazy crap anyway? Jesus in your basement. The president falling down your stairs."

Roger looked down at his hands on the table. "Nobody," he said. "Nobody would believe it."

There was complete quiet. The kind of quiet that can only exist after chaos.

Roger muttered to himself, "I knew this was a bad idea."

Becky lashed out. "Screw you, Roger."

She bolted up from her chair toward the basement door.

"Where are you going?" her husband asked.

"Downstairs to see if He's all right. It probably scared Him to death."

EDWIN 2:2

I EVENTUALLY FOUND MYSELF IN MY pickup truck, driving back in the light rain to the station with Chris Young in the passenger seat. For a time we rode without speaking, alone in our thoughts. Somewhere along the way a conversation started.

Looking out his side window, Chris began, "You said you believed in God. You said you're a Christian. I'm interested to know what you think about all this now. I'm interested to know what you think about this Jesus character."

I didn't answer right away. I'd been wondering the same thing, wallowing around in the ideas, trying hard to reconcile long-held beliefs since the beginning of my memory with the reality of what my eyes had seen.

"Well, I can say this: I don't feel the same as I did a

few days ago."

"What does that mean?"

I explained, "Maybe true faith is blind, but I've never been a man comfortable keeping my eyes closed. I've never seen anything like this before, Chris. I can't prove it, and I can't disprove it. All I know is I'm beginning to feel differently about Him than I felt a few days ago."

We were quiet. The streets were empty. A light rain began to fall. It looked damn cold outside.

"Not me," he said. "I don't feel different about him. I can't reconcile believing just for the sake of believing. Believing because it makes me feel better.

"It reminds me of those people who set their clocks ahead five minutes so they won't be late. They're just fooling themselves. It might be helpful. It might make them feel better to forget for that magical instant when they first see the clock in the morning, but it doesn't change the time. It doesn't change anything."

His voice was low, but it held conviction. He either strongly believed what he said, or he was trying to convince himself.

Chris turned to me, "Tell me this: If God is capable of creating the vastness of space, endless galaxies of planets, suns and moons, why play games with allowing his people, his children, to worship other gods? Why send his son to die on a cross? What's the point of Hell?

"With a snap of his all-powerful fingers, all his children can know and believe in the real God, the real creator of Heaven and Earth. With a blink of an eye he ends all doubts. But instead, he plays cruel games with his children?

"It doesn't make sense, Chief, and the reason it doesn't make sense is because it isn't true, and I'm not willing, just for the sake of feeling more comfortable, to trick myself into thinking it's five minutes later than the truth."

He looked at me for a response. I think he wanted me to say something enlightening. He wanted me to explain it in a way that had never been explained to him before.

I said, "You'd call Becky's belief naïve. I'd call it pure. Me, on the other hand, it might take me a few more bread crumbs to get to the campground, but I don't think it matters how you get there.

"I told you before, my belief in God, my belief in Jesus, is based on my demand, as a man, for nothing less."

Without making a conscious decision to do so, I

started telling the story of my son.

"My wife and I had a baby boy. His name was James. In that single moment, when he was born, everything I felt was important in this world flowed into this baby. Everything.

"I didn't know it was possible. All those things that carried big meaning, like careers, money in the bank, politics, respect in the community, even my marriage and religion, all came together in this little boy.

"I guess that's the way it's supposed to be. I guess the instincts, the animal instincts of survival, survival of yourself and your gene pool, and the entire human species, are so fundamental that instead of everything else being pushed aside, everything else actually comes together. And you can hold it all in your arms, and kiss it on the cheek, and cry for no reason. No damn reason at all."

I stopped and took a slow, deep breath. The rain was the same, no heavier and no lighter. I could feel Chris's eyes on the side of my face and I wondered why I'd started telling this man the story I hadn't told in so many years.

"What happened?" he asked. His voice was soft.

"He died, Chris. He died of cancer. Six years old. It was slow, and horrible, and when he died with me sitting next to him in that hospital bed, everything else died along with him. Everything I had ever cared about. Every cornerstone of this life fell away underneath my feet like dust.

"I hated God. I hated my wife. I hated this job, my house, and mostly I hated myself for not being able to do anything about this shitty, shitty, fucked-up world where a little boy dies for no reason wrapped up in hospital sheets.

"And for months, years, I got out of bed every morning like a robot, and went to work, and ate, and paid bills, because I didn't know what else to do. I can't count how many nights I sat out on my back porch in the dark with a gun in my mouth. But for some reason, and I can't tell you why, I never pulled the trigger. Just sat there, crying, with a gun resting in my mouth, waiting for something."

I pulled the truck into my special parking spot in front of the police station. The windshield wipers slowly traveled across and then back.

"And then one day, Chris, I felt something. It was just a regular day. Maybe a Tuesday.

"I felt something different. I felt hope. It pretty much came out of nowhere. Not like a lightning bolt out of the sky. More like a sunrise, where the light slowly floods across the edge of the world until you can see. My job mattered again. My wife was beautiful to me again."

Chris waited a respectful moment and then asked, "And you think God did that?"

"I do. There's a basic human need for hope. The species needs it like food and water. It sets us apart from the animals."

Chris said, "I agree we need hope like food and water. We need it to survive. That's why we'll create it if necessary. We'll create it out of nothing, like believing in Heaven, or believing in an all-powerful, all-loving God. A God who has sent his only son back to save us from this wretched, hopeless world.

"No disrespect, Chief, but every man needs to be his own God."

I turned off the car. In just a few seconds I could feel the cold, damp air seeping inside. I turned to Chris and said, "I wish I had some great Biblical quote to recite, but I don't. In a way, I suppose we're not so far apart. It's my respect for the individual man, myself, that leads me to accept nothing less than the idea it would take a higher power, a God, to create such a wondrous thing. It's your reverence for men, yourself, that leads you to believe we are all God-like, and so re-

ally, if men are created in God's image as Christians believe, how far away are we from being our own Gods?"

I didn't wait for his answer. I opened the door and
stepped out into the rain. Chris followed me up to the
front door of the station, where we stood under the
eave.

Chris said, "Have you had any luck figuring out
who the second robber might be?"

I sensed the question wasn't random. I sensed he
knew something I didn't know.

"Not yet, " I said. "You got any ideas?"

There was a split second of hesitation. The split
second I'd spent a lifetime in law enforcement learning
to detect. He knew something, but he wasn't willing to
tell me yet.

"No," he said. "No ideas."

The law is patient. I had a few ideas myself, and
time was on my side.

EDWIN 2:3

I SAT IN BED WITH MY wife late that evening. That's what we do. Without making a big production of it, every night before we go to sleep we sit in bed together and talk.

There's a great deal to be said in this life for finding someone who likes to be in your presence. It sounds so simple, but it's not. Just a person, without a private agenda, who genuinely enjoys sitting and talking about anything at all. One person, not at the mercy of the world's mood swings, who not only endures your touch but looks forward to it.

Mary is that person for me.

"WHAT HAPPENED TONIGHT?" SHE ASKED.

"You wouldn't believe it if I told you?"

"I might," she said.

"Okay. The president of the United States and his entourage snuck down here to our little town so the president could have a private meeting with our bank robber in the Sullivans' basement. Apparently, after the meeting, the president fainted, fell down the basement stairs, and ended up being rushed to the emergency room, causing me to lie to the press and tell them one of the Sullivan family members had a medical emergency.

"Whereupon, I drove home with the *New York Times* guy, Chris, and found myself debating whether or not our robber is Jesus Christ in the flesh, with me arguing on the side of yes. And arguing rather well, I must admit."

I turned to Mary for her reaction and wasn't disappointed. She smiled at me the way she's done so many times before.

"I believe you," she said. "Is the president alright?"

"I think he's fine, and by the way, I think Chris knows something about our second robber."

"I guess he's more than just a second robber," she said.

"How's that?"

"He's maybe the one person who can tell the world

that Jesus isn't Jesus, he's just John Doe from Albuquerque, New Mexico. Somebody else's son."

I could feel my police-mind weighing the options.

"I don't think Jesus is going to cooperate, but tomorrow morning I'm gonna call a damn press conference and announce that Jesus has changed His mind and decided to cooperate with the investigation and we've arranged a meeting," I explained. "This might flush him out. If he thinks we're getting ready to figure out who he is, maybe he'll turn himself in or do something stupid."

"Are you sure you want to find him?" she asked.

I hesitated. "Yes," I said.

"Are you sure this Jesus fellow won't help?"

"I've come at Him several times, but I think I'll go over there tomorrow to talk with the man anyway. I'd just like to ask Him a few questions."

We sat quietly for minutes. The house was completely silent.

Mary asked, "What is it that's making you feel differently about this guy? What's different from a few days ago?"

I thought about it.

"Nothing, really. But what would you expect to be different on the outside? Do we have to see a miracle to believe? I mean, one man's miracle is just another man's fortunate accident, right? Everything can be explained away."

She waited for me to finish.

"I don't know, Mary. Maybe I've finally lost my damn mind, but I just feel different around the guy. The longer it goes without proof He isn't Jesus, the more I seem to believe. The less He tries to convince me, the more convinced I become. I know it sounds ridiculous."

I felt her hand touch my shoulder.

"It doesn't sound ridiculous, Edwin."

We sat in silence again. There were times when I knew for sure both of us were thinking about our little boy at the same time. We rarely spoke of him, but the bond between Mary and I had grown solid like a steel beam between us. We didn't usually need to speak of it, but this time was different.

"How often do you think of him?" I asked, resisting the need to look at her.

She moved her hand slowly from my shoulder.

"Every day," she said softly. "I think of him every day. For a while I tried to make myself think of other things. But I don't try to do that anymore. Now, when I think of him, I'm happy I can remember. It's like the memories are God's way of telling me He loves me."

As she spoke, I felt the tears come to my eyes. I'd spent too many years trying to force them away, trying to be a man about it. What a bunch of bullshit. I'm not supposed to cry? Who made up that rule? It couldn't have been the father of a boy who died before his eyes.

"I'm sorry, Mary, that I was gone for a time. I'm sorry that I pulled back so far for so long. I guess everybody eventually learns the limits of their strength, and I learned mine."

I didn't turn to see if she was crying, and I didn't turn away to hide my face.

I drew a long, deep breath.

Mary finally said, "Tomorrow, when you go see Jesus, ask Him if James is waiting for us, and ask Him whether we can be together longer next time."

It made me smile just a bit, thinking of James.

"I'll ask Him," I said.

CHRIS 4:1

I WENT BACK TO MY HOTEL room alone. There was work to do, and for reasons I decided not to fully explore I felt extra energy to find the other guy who robbed the bank. It would be a close to the story, and not just for newspaper purposes. Maybe I couldn't write about the president's visit, but I sure as hell could end the insanity of people believing the foul-smelling, pellet gun bandit was anyone other than another nut roaming around our country without proper medication.

I sat for hours at my computer watching the videotape from the Goodwill store. I stared so long and hard at the grainy footage my eyes began to burn. People in and out, fast-forward, too tall, too short, too fat, and then a man, mid-forties, white, the right height.

I watched him move around the store. He never

went to the dressing room. A baseball cap purchased, baggy pants, and then the shirt so recognizable. The shirt Becky Sullivan remembered taking to the same Goodwill store weeks earlier. The guy even bought a pair of glasses just like the ones worn in the bank that day.

It was him. Unequivocally, it was him. Rewind, forward, stop and start. It was him, the right size, the right age, buying the exact clothes, the day before the robbery.

He looked up at the camera, just once, but it was enough. I printed a picture of the man's face. A normal face, nothing unusual. The picture wasn't perfect, but it was clear enough to identify.

I'd already decided not to go to Becky Sullivan first. She clearly didn't want to help, and if she intentionally lied about the man in the photograph it could eventually hurt the chief's investigation.

So I decided to go to Nick Blankenship. It was mostly a hunch. Why was his name written on that deposit slip? I'd already checked, and Blankenship was about the same age as the robber. He'd grown up here, spent his whole life in this town.

I lay in bed alone hoping to sleep a few hours before the sun rose. There were no sounds to hear, just my heartbeat pounding under my hand resting on my chest.

I was my best when I was alone. As a kid I remember choosing to be by myself, watching, observing, and then thinking. My mother hoped it was a stage, but my need to be alone never changed. It's the only time my thoughts come together in correct sequence, lined up by the laws of reason. The more people, the more chaos. She took me to doctors. One old man even told me I was autistic. He said it explained my fear of social interaction and my love of numbers. Reluctantly, I tried to tell the old man how numbers are easier to understand than people, and much more reliable.

I turned on the television while I got dressed. Chief Bastrop was on the morning news. The question was asked, "Have you made any progress on finding the second robber of the bank?"

"As a matter of fact, we have. The man in custody has decided to cooperate with the investigation. We have a meeting scheduled for tomorrow morning. I anticipate we will make an arrest in the next few days."

The chief hadn't said anything on our late-night drive home about the man in custody agreeing to cooperate. Besides, the defendant had an attorney. Would he cooperate without some sort of deal? And how can you give a deal to a bank robber who won't even reveal his true identity?

The National News Service interrupted. There was a press conference called at the White House. Based on what I'd seen the night before, my first thought was that the president was going to stand up in front of the American people, in front of the world, on a typical Wednesday morning while we sipped our coffee and ate our frozen waffles and announce he'd discovered Jesus Christ.

Instead, Ted Foster stepped up to the microphone. "Nothing to be alarmed about, folks. The president had a fall last night here at the White House. He bumped his head, he's undergoing tests to make sure there aren't any problems. We've been assured by the doctors it's a mild concussion, but I didn't want rumors running wild."

"What happened?" one of the reporters asked.

"I'm told there was some water on the bathroom floor. He just slipped. It might be a while before the president is up and around."

Yeah, I thought. It might be a while before Ted Foster and those boys in Washington let the president anywhere around a reporter or a microphone.

I found Nick Blankenship sitting in his cubicle at

the car dealership. Before he could switch gears from his car salesman persona I put the picture down in front of him.

"Do you know this guy?" I asked quickly.

"Who the hell are you?"

"I'm with the *New York Times*."

"The *New York Times*," he repeated. "The only reason the *New York Times* would be down here is about that stupid son-of-a-bitch who thinks he's Jesus."

I lowered my voice. "Nick, you help me out and maybe there's something in it for you."

"What?" he asked.

I pointed down at the picture. "Do you know who this is?"

He lowered his puffy face down to look closely.

"It looks like a guy named Neil I went to high school with forever ago. I saw him one time a few years ago, at the grocery store I think."

"Neil what?" I asked.

"Neil Bailey, I think. What's he got to do with anything?"

"Probably nothing. Are you sure it's Neil Bailey?"

He lowered his puffy face down again. I didn't have the heart to tell him he was starting to form a bald spot near the crown of his skull.

"Looks like him. Now what exactly is in it for me?"

"I'll let you know, Nick."

I HAD A NAME. I HAD a name, I had a picture, and a guy buying the right clothes at the right place.

Now what to do? Call the chief? No. Go find Neil Bailey? Yes. Because once he got arrested I'd get cut off from the source. He'd be locked up. I'd end up asking all my questions through lawyers. Questions without answers. Maybe I could get the answers before it was too late. I'd go to Neil Bailey's house first.

NEIL 3:1

I HADN'T SLEPT IN FOUR NIGHTS. Literally, hadn't slept. I moved the money from the toolshed to the car, to a hole under the hedges on the side of the house, and then back to the toolshed. I finally decided to burn it all in the fireplace at 3:30 one morning. When all $2,781 was burned into ashes, I started thinking how the FBI could probably test those ashes and find traces of the ink used in currency. So I got down on my hands and knees and cleaned the fireplace like it had never been cleaned before.

While I sat in my favorite brown chair and watched the money burn, there was a false sense of relief, almost like if the money was gone then none of it ever happened. If there was no money, then there was no robbery, and everything could just go back to the way it was before. And then slowly, like smoke rising from the crack beneath a door, I remembered the reason I did it in the first place. I was miserable. Miserable, bored, and lonely in a house full of people. Not just any people, but the people I was closest to in this world. And I was pretty sure they hated my guts. I just wasn't completely sure why.

I was fairly certain it was Wednesday morning. I was sitting alone at the white kitchen table in my t-shirt and bathrobe when Chief Bastrop appeared on the television.

"Have you made any progress on finding the second robber of the bank?" they asked him.

I felt the bile rise from my stomach and little flashes of light appeared in the circle of my field of vision around the TV screen.

"As a matter of fact we have," the chief said with a smirk on his face, like he already knew who I was, and the house was surrounded, and this was just a way to torment me.

"The man in custody has decided to cooperate with the investigation. We have a meeting scheduled for tomorrow morning. I anticipate we will make an arrest in the next few days."

"Jesus Christ," I said out loud. Could they leave me alone? It's not like I shot the president or anything. It's not like I'm Lee Harvey Oswald. The money is gone, burnt, the ashes flushed down the toilet. Probably already been filtered, recycled, and now streaming out somebody's kitchen faucet.

The National News Service interrupted. I half expected an announcement that the president had been assassinated, and I was the shooter, and my picture would flash across the screen with messed-up hair and a sinister look, wearing stupid sunglasses, maybe like a boat captain would wear. Instead, the idiot fell down in his bathroom and hit his pitiful head. I'd trade places with the poor bastard in a heartbeat.

My wife came into the room and sat down at the table across from me. She was dressed sharply, and her hair was pulled back into a tight bun, making her face sort of stretched too tight. I wondered if she'd taken our monthly bill money and got Botox injections.

"I need to talk to you, Neil," she said. I suddenly felt like a child, small and weak, with a grown-up looking down on me with mud on my pants.

"I want a divorce," she said, frankly and dramatically like we were on a TV show, but no one had told me my lines.

I couldn't stop staring at her face, particularly the skin around her eyes pulled so tight. If she had Botox, would I be able to see the needle marks?

"It's been a long time since I've been happy, Neil. A long time. Let's face it, we're very different people. We want very different things in life."

"Like what?" I asked curiously.

"What do you mean?" she snapped.

I explained. "Like what do you want in life that I don't want?"

Her eyes thinned. The skin seemed to tighten even further.

"Well," she said, "for example: I've wanted to be a member at the country club forever. And you don't care. You just don't care. If you cared about me and the girls, you'd do whatever it took to give that to us, but you don't. You simply don't, because we're different people, and we want different things. I have no idea what you want."

In just a few sentences I went from feeling like that little boy scolded by the mean lady next door to imagining in fine detail blowing her fuckin' brains all over the kitchen walls with my pistol. I could even see the bloody bits in a pattern on the cream-colored wallpaper behind her head.

"And the girls feel the same as I do. In fact, they both came to me and told me I should file for divorce. They're very smart girls, you know."

I just stared at her. There was no expression, no movement.

We sat for the longest time across our kitchen table from each other like strangers at a cafeteria. It occurred to me we were worse than strangers. We were people who once loved each other, conceived children together, and held hands at a theater, but now we were enemies, consumed slowly by the deep hatred only years can allow.

"Well," she said, "are you going to say anything?"

I thought about it for a moment.

"No."

She waited there a while longer. I'm not sure she knew why. Then she got up and left the same way she arrived.

I took off my wedding ring and set it in the exact middle of the white table. From where I sat I could see the ring from a different angle, a different perspective than I'd seen it all those years. The silver was weathered and dull, but the tiny black braids around the edges still held their definition.

Seeing the ring alone in the middle of the table, it was hard to believe that I'd ever worn it.

NEIL 3:2

A BEAM OF SUNLIGHT EDGED THROUGH the blinds on the kitchen window and illuminated the white table slowly until I was surrounded in light. The sound of the front door slamming snapped me back into the day. The house was empty and there was relief in the emptiness.

I started to think again of the list of possible loose ends. The pellet gun was at the bottom of a lake, untraceable back to me. The money was gone, the ink-filled ashes all flushed away. By now the clothes, hat, and glasses had been hauled from the Dumpster. It was only Jesus. He was the only loose end, and the words of Chief Bastrop echoed in my head:

"The man in custody has decided to cooperate with the investigation. We have a meeting scheduled tomorrow morning. I anticipate we will make an arrest in the next few days."

I inched my hand down and felt the cold pistol resting in my lap. I hadn't left the house without it in days. It held a quieting security. It held answers. Final answers, if necessary.

BAM, BAM, BAM.

There was a knock on the front door. The knock of a man, loud and purposeful.

I sat upright in my chair and waited, the bile rising again.

A few seconds later, *BAM, BAM, BAM.*

The same knuckles against my door. The same knock.

I stood in my bathrobe and clutched the pistol tightly. I circled slowly on weak legs to the window in the dining room that gave me a view to the front yard.

A man, a black man, with a button-down blue shirt walked from my front porch down the driveway to a red car. The car looked like a rental, and the man was a man I'd never seen before.

Could he be FBI? Could he be one of Chief Bastrop's men? A new guy maybe, an investigator brought in for the robbery? Or maybe just someone lost, knocking at the door of the wrong house?

The black man stopped at his car door and looked back at the house. I jerked away from the window and waited for the car to start and the sound of him pulling away. My eyes closed, and I slid down the wall slowly until I sat alone on the cool hardwood floor of the dining room.

I needed something to eat. I needed to get out of the house before something bad happened. Before the man came back and beat on my door, or showed up with a search warrant and twenty wide-eyed officers.

I got myself dressed and put the gun gently in the space under the car seat as I pulled away. It was strange to look at my house from the street. It didn't look like my house anymore, just another house on another block in another make-believe neighborhood. It was unrecognizable, just like my life.

I roamed around the grocery store picking up odd things that looked good. For some reason I really wanted an apple, a green apple, shiny, inviting, the promise of tart juice inside.

I stood in line to check out. I was aware of a person behind me, a woman, looking at me. I turned to see. Weakness invaded my legs. It was the red-headed bank teller. It was the woman with the off-centered eyes who placed her hand on the deposit slip that morning as we had a tiny tug-of-war over the little piece of paper with Nick Blankenship's name written across the top.

Why had I written his name? Why had a random kid I knew in high school so many years earlier come to mind at such a critical moment? Why had I given the police a sample of my handwriting?

Our eyes met for an instant. I turned away and felt like I might lose my balance.

"Sir?"

I almost fell to the floor, catching myself.

It was the girl at the cash register,

"Sir," she repeated, "cash or charge?"

"Cash," I said.

As I fumbled for my wallet, I could feel the red-headed woman behind me leaning to put her items on the black conveyor belt, leaning to see the side of my face, and I turned ever so slightly to deny her the view.

I tried to walk casually out the door, and then hurried to my car. I threw the few groceries in the passenger seat and felt for the gun, resting it back in my lap, and then waited to watch the woman leave the store. The green apple rolled loose from the bag onto the car floor and came to rest in the farthest corner, just beyond my reach.

Her eyes scanned the parking lot, and I lowered

myself down in the seat. She pushed her cart out to a greenish minivan parked several rows away. I watched as the woman unloaded the groceries, her eyes still glancing about, pushing her hair back from her misshapen face.

When the minivan pulled out from the lot, I started the car and followed a good distance behind. She drove slowly, and for a second I wondered if it was all a setup. Was this how they would catch me? Was this how they'd get their ID before making the arrest?

I looked back and forth in my mirrors, on the side and behind. Nothing. No one suspicious. The apple rolled slowly from one side of the floor to the other.

The minivan turned right, and I turned right. A few miles away eventually she put on her blinker and pulled into a driveway. I could see a news van parked on the street ahead.

I stopped several hundred yards back. I knew from the news reports she was the woman who'd posted the bond for Jesus, and he was staying at her house. I'd seen the house on the news and clips of Jesus with his ankle bracelet walking up the front steps into her home.

He was there, inside her house, only a few hundred yards away, and I thought how easy it would be to put the gun to my temple, count to three, and put an end to this torment. It was only a few seconds away, a few seconds of vacant thought and everything would be simple.

BECKY 2:1

I T WAS SO WEIRD TO SEE that man in the grocery store. There was something about the side of his face that reminded me of the man in the bank that day. I tried to get a better look, and I could swear he kept turning away so I couldn't see him good.

He wasn't wearing a wedding ring though, and the wedding ring is what I remembered the best. Since the bank robber was wearing a hat and glasses, I couldn't be sure. Besides, what difference does it make? Nobody got hurt. It was the best day of my whole life. If it wasn't for that day I wouldn't know my purpose.

Since Jesus moved into my basement, I've tried to walk very quietly around the house. The kids stomping in the kitchen made a lot of racket down below. I never paid much attention to it before, but then every stomp made me worry. Every creak of the floor sent my blood pressure up.

My teeth clenched together. "Quiet. You have to be quiet, Roger," I said again.

"This is my house, Becky. I can stomp if I want to."

"It's not your house anymore, Roger. It's the house of the Lord. If you can't be quiet you'll find yourself sleeping at your mama's. Why aren't you at work, anyway?"

"I took a vacation day. This is stupid. The man robbed a bank. He's not Jesus. He's just a guy you've let take over our house."

I punched Roger in the chest so hard it felt like my fist stuck through his skin and landed directly against the bone in the middle.

I could feel the fury in my face. "Shut your mouth or leave this house."

The door from the basement opened and Jesus stepped out.

"Is everybody okay?" He asked. "I heard voices."

Roger said, "No, everything is not okay."

"Shhh," I said. "Everything's fine. I'm making lasagna for supper."

Roger said, "We just had lasagna. See, everything's not fine."

I tried to hide my anger. "It's Jesus' favorite. He loves lasagna. We're going to have it tonight."

There was a knock on the front door. I welcomed the interruption and left the room. There was no choice between Roger and Jesus. Roger would lose every time. He was stupid if he didn't understand it.

I opened the door to see the black man from the *New York Times*. The TV people and the cameras had mostly left our front yard, but a few hadn't given up. Every now and then one would come back, film a reporter saying a few things with our house in the background, and then leave. My boys thought it was funny to hide in the bushes and throw rocks at the vans. I thought it was funny too, until one of those rocks busted out a window and a lady told us we would have to pay for it.

"Hello, Becky," the *New York Times* man said.

"Hello."

"Do you have a minute? I wanted to show you something."

I stepped out on the porch and closed the door behind.

"What?" I asked.

He unfolded a piece of paper with a picture of a man's face. It was the man from the grocery store.

"Do you recognize this guy?"

I looked harder at the picture. Sometimes my bad eye plays tricks on my good eye, but most of the time I can close the bad one and the good one works just fine.

"Why?" I asked.

"I think it might be the second robber."

"Why do you want to find him so bad?"

the *New York Times* man didn't answer. He just stood there.

I said, "Why?"

"Well," he started, "I think it might help us figure out who the man living in your basement really is."

"I already know who He is, and the president, a man a lot smarter than you, knows, too. I just heard on the radio they rescheduled his press conference for tomorrow morning.

"Tomorrow morning the president is going to tell everybody in this country that Jesus Christ, our Lord and Savior, is living in my house. Do you know what that means?"

The big-shot man from the *New York Times* looked like he was afraid of me. He looked like Roger looked when I punched a hole in his fat chest.

"Becky," he said, "do you recognize the man in the picture?"

I looked at him square in the face. "No. I don't. And you need to leave this house before something bad happens to you."

We stared at each other.

"What do you mean?" he asked.

"Just what I said. There're two sides: the good side, and the bad side, the believers and the doubters. You better figure out where you stand because after tomorrow nothing else matters. Your fancy job doesn't matter. My boss, Mr. Tinsely, doesn't matter. How pretty you are, how rich you are, none of it matters."

I felt strong. I felt stronger than I had ever felt before. I turned around and closed the front door behind me, leaving the man standing on my porch holding his limp picture.

BECKY 2:2

I WENT BACK TO THE KITCHEN. Jesus and Roger were sitting at the table eating cinnamon rolls with the boys. Eric, my youngest, was picking his nose.

"Stop that," I said, and caught myself in time to correct my tone of voice. "We don't pick our noses at the table. It's gross."

The lawyer, Jay Mason, walked straight in the front door without knocking. His shoes stomped across the floor.

"Was that the guy from the *New York Times* just leaving? You didn't give the bastard a story, did you? I've been on the phone all night. We've got exclusives lined up. Don't give nothing away for free."

"I didn't tell him anything," I said. "I told him to leave."

"Good," Jay said.

He looked like he'd slept the night in his car. Even a fancy car is no place to sleep. Jay's eyes were red, and he held an unlit cigarette in his hand. His shirt was unbuttoned too far and there was nasty black chest hair peeking out.

He sat down in the only empty chair at the table and said to Jesus, "Did you see Bastrop's press conference this morning? He says you're cooperating with him. He says he's got a meeting with you tomorrow to give up your co-defendant. Don't you think maybe you could let me know what's going on?"

Jesus took another bite of his cinnamon roll. "I don't know what you're talking about."

Jay continued, "I'm not saying it's a bad idea. I mean, if they offered probation or something, maybe we could play that card."

Jay shoved his hand deep in his pocket and pulled out two little blue pills. He swallowed them down with Eric's orange juice.

"Do you see what I am saying?" he asked.

Roger said, "The president was here last night."

"The president of what?" Jay asked.

"The president of the United States. He came to see your friend," and Roger pointed at Jesus.

"Bullshit," Jay said. He started to light his cigarette. I was going to tell him no, but seeing that he's a lawyer and all I didn't say anything. I just watched, but I didn't like the way he was acting.

"No, really," Roger said. "He showed up here out of nowhere with a bunch of Secret Service guys just to meet in private downstairs with the famous Jesus Bandit who loves my wife's lasagna."

"You've got to be kidding me," Jay said, and then he turned to Jesus. "What did you tell him?"

Jesus said softly, "Nothing, really. We just talked and then he fell down the stairs."

Jay lost track of the conversation. "I'm going to be at that meeting tomorrow. You understand? I'm gonna be there."

"There is no meeting," Jesus said.

"Don't try to cut me out, you hear me?" Jay pointed his finger at Jesus in a mean way. I couldn't stand it anymore.

"You need to leave, Jay," I said.

"What?"

"You need to leave my home."

Jay leaned back in his chair. "Oh, I understand. You've got another lawyer. Somebody got to you. It won't be that easy you know, cuttin' me out. We're blood. It's a big mistake. Big mistake. You mark my words."

Jay seemed to drift away again, and then he just stood up and walked out the door. Roger slammed down his cinnamon roll and ran out after him, the boys following close behind, all of them stomping.

It was just me and Jesus alone in the kitchen. I could hear voices in the yard.

"I'm sorry," I said.

"Sorry for what?"

"Sorry for the way they treat you."

"You can't be sorry for what others do, Becky. As a man thinks in his heart, so is he."

I sat down next to Him at the table. As before, being in His presence made me feel calm and sure. When we were alone, it was like there was no one else alive, just the two of us, me and Jesus. He made all other men seem disgusting and small.

His hands rested on the table next to the white plate. I wanted so much to touch Him. I wanted so much to put my hand on His, and He seemed to understand what I wanted.

I took my hand from my lap and stretched it across to where Jesus' hand rested on the table, and gently placed my hand on top of His.

It was like warm water flowed from Him into me, through my fingers, into my arm, and through my whole body. It was like I was immersed in a bath, and we didn't move. Neither of us moved. The warmth reached every part of me. I'll never know why, but I asked Him, "Do you think I'm pretty?"

It was the dumbest thing to say, but at the time, at the very moment, I asked Jesus if I was pretty, when I knew, and I'd always known, the answer.

"Yes, Becky," He said. "Yes, you are pretty."

The front door slammed with a crash, and I pulled my hand away from His and turned my face to the empty wall.

EDWIN 3:1

SITTING AT MY OFFICE IN THE police station I looked at the clock next to the framed picture of my wife. Frank Perry, my enthusiastic young investigator, sat across from me.

"I keep running into dead ends", he said. "I sure as hell hope this works. The more I think about it, the more I think the other robber is local, so maybe if he thinks his buddy's about to rat him out it might shake something loose."

"You never know," I said.

"At least the press coverage has died down a little bit. There were only three or four of them outside when I got here this morning," Frank said.

I said, "If you wait long enough, something else will get their attention. They're kinda like dogs always chas-

ing the next squirrel, or the next car that goes by. Somebody somewhere will shoot up a school, or a movie star
will get themselves arrested, and then Jesus becomes a
back-page story, and eventually no story of all."

Frank Perry added, "I can't wait until we ID that
son-of-a-bitch. I can't wait until we can stand up in
court in front of everybody and make him look like a
fool for acting like he's Jesus, and then watch him go
to prison where he belongs. I don't think those boys in
prison will appreciate his act."

I could see Frank's face harden as he spoke. He was
angry, just like Becky Sullivan was angry when her beliefs were questioned. Why is it the fanatics, on one side
or the other, are always so damn sure of themselves,
while the thoughtful men dance with their doubts?

I said, "I'm going over to the Sullivan house in a
few minutes to see Him."

"Why?" Frank Perry asked.

"I want to talk to the man, alone. Besides, maybe
he needs a little police protection."

"Do you think you can get him to tell you about
his buddy?"

"I'm not going to ask Him," I said.

"What?"

"I'm not going to ask Him about his buddy. I just

want to talk to Him about other things."

Frank Perry leaned up in his chair. "You're not falling for his crap, are you, Chief? You're not believing this man is Jesus?"

When I didn't answer, Frank said, "Why did the president of the United States come all the way down here to meet with him? Why would he waste his time?"

"I don't know, Frank. I wasn't part of their conversation."

"If you ask me, I think it's bullshit. I heard on the TV the president has some big press conference scheduled for tomorrow morning. Do you think it's got anything to do with this?"

"I don't know, maybe," I said. "If the president stood up on TV at the White House and announced our bank robber is Jesus Christ, and each of us needs to get right with the Lord because He's come back just like the Bible said He would, would you believe it then?"

"Hell, no," Frank said, still leaning up in his chair, red-faced.

"What if the preachers and priests, even the minister at your church told you it was true—what then?"

Frank just stared at me across the desk.

"Ask yourself, Frank, what would it take for you to believe?"

He looked at me like it was the first time he'd thought of such a thing, and then he stood up without a word and walked out the door of my office.

I looked back at the clock next to the picture of my wife. In a few minutes I'd drive to Becky Sullivan's house and sit down on the back porch and talk to this man who calls himself Jesus.

As I walked past Frank in his cubicle, he looked at me, and shot, "He could take a walk on water. How about that? That would be better than robbing a bank."

I could have answered, but I didn't.

EDWIN 3:2

I DROVE ALONE IN MY TRUSTY old blue pickup truck to Becky Sullivan's neighborhood. It was like most neighborhoods in our town, not too fancy and not too poor, somewhere in the middle.

When I pulled into the driveway there were still two or three press people camped out. Linda, the woman from Channel 5 who first called me minutes after the robbery and coined the phrase "Jesus Bandit," hurried from her car to meet me, cameraman in tow.

"You said your meeting wasn't until tomorrow morning," she barked.

"That's right."

"What are you doing here?"

"Just checking on our defendant. Just making sure everybody's safe and sound."

The light on the camera kicked on and Linda asked, "Have there been threats against the Jesus Bandit, Chief Bastrop?"

She shoved the microphone through the open truck window.

"No, Linda, there haven't, but I suppose if there were it might be a better story."

Linda shook her head and the camera light kicked off. They walked away from me, nothing else to talk about, and I made may way to the front door.

After I knocked I heard Roger's voice inside say, "Who the hell is it now?"

A few seconds later Becky opened the door with a jerk. No matter how many times I saw her, I just couldn't get used to her face. The lack of symmetry, almost like halves of two different faces, made it impossible to feel comfortable. It occurred to me she'd spent her entire life seeing the uneasiness in the eyes of everyone she met. I wondered, after all these years, how she saw her own face in the mirror each morning. Like the rest of us, did she slowly stop seeing herself, or was the deformation so profound in her own eyes that she walked away from the mirror each morning with the same denial?

"Can I come in, Becky?" I asked.

"Hey, Chief."

She opened the door as her two crazy-ass children sprinted past, the older boy beating the younger boy with an orange plastic baseball bat across the back of his buzz-cut head. The younger one screamed as loud as I've ever heard a human scream, and at a pitch that made my ears actually hurt deep inside.

"Go to your room," Becky yelled in a tone my mother had never used with me and my sister, but of course we never screamed with a pitch capable of bursting eardrums.

I followed Becky into the kitchen, where Roger was sitting quietly. It was nearly lunchtime and Becky was mixing something in a bowl near the stove.

"Good morning, Roger," I said.

Roger looked pissed about something. "You're not talking to him, Chief, without his lawyer present. That's the law."

"You're right, Roger. It would be a violation of his constitutional rights to talk to him about the robbery or anything pertaining to the robbery of the bank. Would it be too much to ask for a cup of coffee?"

Without speaking, Becky poured me a cup.

"Black is fine," I said. "I just stopped by to say hello. I didn't come for an interrogation."

Roger said, still agitated, "And what's the big announcement he's cooperating with the investigation and giving up the other bank robber, if there is one?"

"Just seeing if maybe we can smoke him out. Just a little police work."

Roger said, "I think it's shitty."

"Roger, you probably think most things are shitty right now. I imagine this is all a pretty big inconvenience, but it won't last forever."

Roger said, "You're damn right it won't last forever."

Becky wheeled around and yelled, "Just shut up, Roger. Shut your mouth."

She stared at her husband across the room until he got up from his chair and walked down a hallway out of sight.

"I'm sorry," she said to me.

"Don't be sorry for what other people do," I said.

"That's the same thing Jesus told me, Chief."

She looked like she might cry, and then she said, "You believe it's Him, don't you? You believe He's Jesus, I know you do."

I couldn't look at her face, so I raised the cup to my lips and focused on the first hot sip of black coffee.

"Where is He?" I asked.

She turned slowly back to her mixing bowl. "On the back porch. He likes to sit out there in the rocking chair. I guess He's got a lot to think about."

"I suppose so," I said.

We stayed in the kitchen for several minutes without speaking. I could hear the crazy-ass kids fighting in a back bedroom. It sounded like one of them stuck his head through the sheetrock wall.

I walked slowly to the back door and saw Jesus through the glass, sitting alone in the rocking chair where she said He'd be. There was an empty chair next to Him, and I walked out and sat down.

It was an overcast day, not too cool and not too hot. There was a little breeze, the kind that blows in a cool front.

Jesus looked at me.

I casually asked, "You drink coffee?"

"Sometimes," He said. "It makes me jittery."

"I know what you mean."

We both rocked gently. The backyard was surrounded by a hedge of bushes that came all the way up to the edge of the covered porch. The hedges were thick, but I could see the top of the house behind where the president and his men had gathered before coming for their visit. Kids' toys were littered around the back steps, a beat-up bicycle and a flat soccer ball.

Jesus said, "You didn't come here to talk about coffee."

"Don't worry," I said, "I won't ask you any incriminating questions without your lawyer present."

"I'm not worried," He said, and He clearly wasn't. The man was very much at ease in the rocking chair, His large, rough hands resting on each arm of the chair.

"Then what did you come to talk to me about?" He asked.

I wasn't nervous. I thought I'd be, but I wasn't. We sat and rocked awhile, and there was a serenity I hadn't felt in a long time.

I started to talk. "My wife and I had a son, James, who died when he was six years old. I've had a hard time understanding why. I mean, why would a little boy have to suffer like that? Why would my wife and I have to watch our child suffer and die before our eyes?"

I felt myself begin to cry. I felt myself begin to let go and cry the way a man never does. It came up from inside so quickly and so completely I just let it happen. The tears rolled down my face, and I didn't wipe them away. I thought of James that last day.

"Daddy, hold my hand," he said.

"Daddy, am I going to die?"

And I lied to him. *"No, baby, you're not going to die."*

"I shouldn't have lied," I said to Jesus.

"I shouldn't have lied to him. I should have trusted. I should have carried him gently and not held on for my own selfishness."

The cool breeze drifted across my face, making the tears cold on my skin, but there was no shame. A light drizzle began to fall.

"Forgive yourself," He said. "Because James has already forgiven you. He's waiting, Edwin. He's waiting for you and his mother, and this time you'll be together for as long as you wish."

He reached his hand across and rested it on the top of mine. I felt the touch, and then I felt the warmth. I can only say it was like the sensation of putting your hand in warm water, and the feeling traveled up my arm and into my body, flooding me with a peace I knew would never leave me in this life.

Jesus said, "Sometimes I feel like giving up."

We rocked gently, and the light rain fell quietly on the tin roof above us. Jesus took His hand from mine and placed it back on His chair. My coffee cup was empty.

After a while, I stood and said, "I'm gonna get another cup. You want one?"

"No thanks," He said.

I walked back inside and poured another cup of coffee standing next to Becky Sullivan in her kitchen. From the back room I heard one of the boys yell, "Shit," at the top of his lungs.

Becky didn't miss a beat in her mixing bowl.

NEIL 4:1

I'M NOT SURE HOW LONG I sat in my car parked down the street from the Sullivan house. I was thinking about Nick Blankenship, searching the file cabinet of school memories, grade by grade, to see if there was anything to explain the way he popped into my head in the bank.

I couldn't find anything. I could barely place a face with the name. For whatever reason I didn't like the guy, but for the life of me I couldn't remember why. Just another person passing by in the flow of life.

It didn't matter. Nothing much matters. There wasn't anything to go home to.

I started the car and headed down the street slowly. The Channel 5 news van was parked outside the Sullivan house. As I passed, Chief Bastrop stepped out of a pickup truck and looked directly at me for an instant before he turned to move toward the house.

I'd just seen the man earlier in the morning on TV saying his meeting wasn't until tomorrow. Was it a lie? Was it another police trick to make me feel safe for one more day as they closed in? The bastards were scheming. Jesus was probably part of it. Everybody had a role.

Who the hell did he think he was, anyway? Did he really believe anybody was stupid enough to buy the Jesus act?

I took a right turn, and then another, ending up at the house on the other side of the block behind the home of Becky Sullivan. The house looked empty. There were no cars in the driveway. The mailbox hung upside down on the side of its post. Some of the numbers had fallen off.

It was like I wasn't really making decisions anymore. It was like the decisions were being made for me, and I was floating on a steady current going slowly in a direction I'd never been.

I got out of my car and walked around the side of the empty house. There was a tall hedge of bushes along the backyard boardering the Sullivan house, and I went to the right slowly on the side of the hedge.

There were voices. I couldn't hear the words, but

they were the voices of men, two men, and as I inched closer the voices belonged to Jesus and the police chief.

A light rain began to fall. Through the tall hedge I could see toys and junk around the backyard under a rusty basketball goal. There was a bicycle leaning against the handrail of the back steps leading up to the two men sitting side by side in rocking chairs under the roof of the porch.

Water rolled down my forehead. Sweat, rain, a combination of the two, cold on my skin. I was maybe twenty feet away, completely hidden from their view.

The chief was crying, almost like a child. His voice shook.

"I shouldn't have lied to him," he said. "I should have trusted. I should have carried him gently and not held on for my own selfishness."

And then Jesus, in a voice full of himself, said, "Forgive yourself, because James has already forgiven you. He's waiting, Edwin. He's waiting for you and his mother, and this time you'll be together for as long as you wish."

I felt angry. I felt angry that a man like the chief of police would listen to this shit and act like the words were anything more than just words. I felt angry I was standing hidden in the bushes with the cold rain falling on my head while they sat warm in rocking chairs, just rocking like the world was right, back and forth like any regular day.

Jesus said, "Sometimes I feel like giving up."

I felt the weight of the pistol hanging in my hand like I hadn't even noticed it was there. I thought of my wife at the kitchen table, so dismissive. Her face, the way she walked away from me.

The chief said, "I'm gonna get another cup. You want one?"

"No thanks," I heard, and then there was the sound of the back door closing.

I stepped out from behind the bushes and stood at the bottom of the steps with the gun pointed directly at the chest of Jesus, rocking slowly in his chair.

He didn't move. He didn't change his face. It was like he already knew. It was like, in that very moment, he expected me to step out from behind the tall hedges and stand in front of him with a gun in my hand pointed at his chest ten feet away, a child's bicycle next to me, toys at my feet.

And in those few seconds of vacant thought, those few empty seconds, I pulled the trigger and ended it all, just like He knew I'd do.

Just like both of us knew all along.

ABOUT THE AUTHOR

Frank Turner Hollon lives in Alabama with his wife and children. He is the author of *The God File*, *A Thin Difference*, *The Point Of Fracture*, *The Wait*, and *Life Is A Strange Place*, which was developed into the movie Barry Munday. Frank is currently assisting with the screenplay for his novel *blood & circumstance*, scheduled to begin filming this year.